Destination Brides

Will the trip of a lifetime lead to the altar?

When Molly, Maya, Jenna and Eve bid on bucket-
list-worthy vacations at a charity auction, they each
embark on the adventure of a lifetime at glamorous
destinations around the world—but will they find
love that lasts forever along the way?

Travel with them from the comfort of your armchair in

Summer Escape with the Tycoon by Donna Alward

Swept Away by the Venetian Millionaire by Nina Singh

One Night in Provence by Barbara Wallace

All available now!

And look out for

Eve's story by Liz Fielding

Available September!

Dear Reader,

This series started as a text conversation. Donna Alward, Nina Singh, Liz Fielding and I decided we wanted to write a miniseries involving exotic, once-in-a-lifetime vacations. Getting to work together was a bucket-list item for us, so it made perfect sense we send our heroines on bucket-list adventures.

I knew immediately that my book would be set in Provence. I wanted my heroine to go somewhere breathtakingly romantic, and what could be more breathtaking than miles and miles of flowers in a land that has seen thousands of years of history. (Yeah, you're going to find a lot of me in my hero, Philippe.)

Throughout writing this book, I jokingly referred to it as my death book, because it involves a hospice nurse and an orphaned hero. Really, though, it's a book about life. Or rather, about *living*. Both Jenna and Philippe are alive, but they aren't living life to the fullest. That's because they are afraid to love and be loved.

An unplanned pregnancy changes everything, however.

This book has a little bit of everything in it, including French lavender fields, Roman ruins, rocky New England beaches and romantic sunsets. I hope it leaves you yearning for a bucket-list adventure of your own.

Drop me an email at Barbara@BarbaraWallace.com and let me know what you think.

Regards,

Barbara Wallace

One Night in Provence

Barbara Wallace

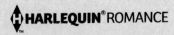

ISBN-13: 978-1-335-49947-9

One Night in Provence

First North American publication 2019

Copyright © 2019 by Barbara Wallace

Printed in U.S.A.

www.Harlequin.com

Barbara Wallace can't remember when she wasn't dreaming up love stories in her head, so writing romances for Harlequin Romance is a dream come true. Happily married to her own Prince Charming, she lives in New England with a house full of empty-nest animals. Occasionally her son comes home, as well! To stay up-to-date on Barbara's news and releases, sign up for her newsletter at barbarawallace.com.

Books by Barbara Wallace

Harlequin Romance

The Men Who Make Christmas

Christmas with Her Millionaire Boss

Royal House of Corinthia

Christmas Baby for the Princess
Winter Wedding for the Prince

The Vineyards of Calanetti

Saved by the CEO

In Love with the Boss

A Millionaire for Cinderella
Beauty & Her Billionaire Boss

The Billionaire's Fair Lady
The Courage to Say Yes
The Man Behind the Mask
Swept Away by the Tycoon
The Unexpected Honeymoon
Their Christmas Miracle

Visit the Author Profile page
at Harlequin.com for more titles.

For Jenna, Shirley and Donna (the real ones).
I couldn't have gotten through this without you.

And, as always, for my hero, Pete. I love you.

Praise for
Barbara Wallace

CHAPTER ONE

Early August

Is the place as gorgeous as it looked in the brochure? Wait, don't tell me. I don't want to know. Tell me it's horrible.

SUNSHINE WARMED JENNA'S face as she read her friend's text. Setting down her champagne, she quickly snapped a photo, knowing the camera phone could never do justice to the Provençal sea of gold and lavender. Her phone dinged in response almost immediately.

I hate you.

Jenna snorted. She shouldn't laugh. Poor Shirley was back in Nantucket with shingles instead of sitting here in the sunshine with her.

She quickly typed a response.

Would it make you feel better if I told you everyone looks like a swimsuit model? I'm the pastiest person here.

That wasn't exactly true. There were definitely some gorgeous people floating around, but there were plenty of pale tourists like Jenna as well. What was a little white lie, though, if thinking her best friend felt out of place made Shirley feel a little better?

I'm not going to have nearly as much fun without you with me.

That *was* true. Shirley was her wing person, both at the nursing home where they worked and off duty. In fact, it was Shirley who'd heard about the Merchant charity auction and convinced Jenna to bid on this Provençal vacation. Without her, Jenna wouldn't be sitting on the terrace of a centuries-old French castle drinking champagne for breakfast.

Better double down on your efforts, then. Otherwise, Beatrice will come back to haunt you. She expected you to have as much fun as possible.

I plan to!

No way was she risking the posthumous wrath of her favorite patient.

Unfortunately, I've lost my translator.

Shirley was the one who could speak French. An ex-boyfriend had given her an immersion software course one Christmas with the promise of a French vacation.

Besides, there's only so much trouble a person can get into by themselves.

A trio of bouncing dots on her screen indicated that Shirley was typing a reply.

Go find a sexy Frenchman to help you. I can think of plenty of trouble you can get into with one of those.

Jenna laughed out loud, causing the couple at the next table to look over. She waved her phone at them to show she wasn't some random crazy person before replying.

R U kidding? With my luck it'll be some poser.

You think everyone is a poser.

With good reason. Nantucket attracted them like a magnet. Thirty K millionaires, she and Shirley liked to call them. Guys with rented boats and empty bank accounts who spent their summer weekends pretending they were part of the beautiful people with the hopes of scoring with as many women as possible.

The South of France isn't the White Whale Tavern.

It's probably worse. I'd rather be haunted by Beatrice, thank you.

Shirley responded by sending a GIF of a dancing ghost.

If you do find a Frenchman, let me know. If I'm going to be covered in sores, I need some kind of vicarious thrill.

Don't hold your breath.

I never do.

After a few more exchanges, Shirley signed off to go back to sleep, it being early morning in New England. Jenna signaled the server for a second glass of champagne. Because when in France...

On the other side of the terrace railing, the landscape rolled out like a sea of purple, green and yellow. A picture postcard come to life, only better.

Ten days in a French castle at the height of lavender season. That's how Merchant Hotels had described the dream package Jenna bid on at the auction. The accompanying brochures made the trip sound magical. Now that she was here, she realized the pictures didn't begin to do the magic justice.

She raised her glass in honor of the woman who'd made the trip possible. "Thanks for the adventure, Beatrice. I'll make the most of it."

Lifting the glass just a bit higher, she snapped a picture and sent the shot to Shirley. Then she switched seats so she could get a photograph of her drinking with the fields behind her. If she was going to rub salt in Shirley's wounds, then she might as well rub a lot of salt.

Unfortunately, she was the only millennial alive who couldn't shoot a decent selfie. She either looked like she was squinting at the sky or like she had two extra chins. After four aborted attempts, she gave up and tossed the phone on the table.

A shadow crossed her table. *"Excusez-moi de vous déranger,"* said a deep voice, "but would you care for some assistance?"

Ho. Ly. Cow. Shirley would be choking on her champagne right now. Jenna nearly did. She was looking at quite possibly the most gorgeous man she'd ever seen. He stood at the ready in a double-breasted suit similar to what the other hotel managers wear wearing, looking like someone plucked him from a hotel brochure. In fact, Château de Beauchamp should put him in the brochure; they'd probably triple their reservation rate. Who knew jaws that chiseled existed in real life?

Granted, he was a tad on the lean side, but then who needed muscles when you could wear a suit with style and had eyes the color of the fields outside?

And…she was staring. As though she'd never seen a handsome man before.

Not this handsome, a voice whispered in her head.

He knew he was handsome, too. She could tell from the way he smiled, his teeth all white and perfect.

"Your camera," he said in heavily-accented

English. "I couldn't help noticing your frustration. I would be glad to take your photograph, if you'd like. You are trying to take a photo in front of the lavender, are you not?"

From the way he focused all his attention on her, you would think there was nothing else he would rather do than help her with her vacation shots. Her stomach fluttered, and she had to remind herself this was France's—or rather the Merchant Hotel chain's—version of five-star service.

"Thank you," she said. "I'm afraid I don't have the selfie trick down yet."

"That is a good thing, is it not? Means you're busy looking at things other than yourself."

Smooth, the way he threw in the compliment. "I'm trying to break that habit on this trip. My friend Shirley was unable to come, so I want to document everything so I can show her when I get home."

"Well, you won't find a better backdrop in all of Provence than this one right here," he replied. "Why don't you stand by the rail? The view is its most breathtaking up close."

Jenna would call him biased, except that he might be right. She'd never seen so much color in one place. Maybe it was an effect brought on by the champagne, but everything seemed more vivid here. The lavender's purple deeper, the sunflowers' gold more brilliant. Even the mountains, with their shadows, looked like they were bathed in blue and green.

"You're American," her photographer noted. "Is this your first visit to Château de Beauchamp?"

"Yes, it is." First time to the château. First time to France. First time outside the United States since spring break in college. "I couldn't resist the idea of staying in a real-life castle. Especially one that's a thousand years old. America wasn't even a gleam in Columbus's eye then."

"I hate to disappoint you, but you've been shortchanged by a few hundred years."

"What do you mean?"

He joined her at the railing. As he eased his way around the chair, Jenna noted the fluid grace with which he moved. Like water rounding a bend.

"This isn't the original castle," he told her.

"But the brochure said the Château de Beauchamp had stood watch over the valley since the eleventh century. Were they making that up?" If the hotel misled her, she was going to be really ticked off.

"*A* Château de Beauchamp has stood guard,"

he replied. "Just not this one. The original fell into ruin sometime in the sixteenth century. If you look beyond that clump of trees to the right, you'll see the remains of the tower."

A gold signet ring on his pinkie finger glittered in the sun as he pointed. Squinting, Jenna made out the peaks of toppled stone.

"The d'Usay family built this as a replacement. They called it the *Château Neuf.*"

"So I'm staying in a five-hundred-year-old castle instead of a thousand-year-old one."

"I trust you're not too disappointed?"

"I'll survive."

"I hope so. It would be a shame if you were left unsatisfied."

Damn, if the double entendre didn't send a quiver through her. If it was a double entendre. The jet lag had thrown her instincts off.

"Have you taken the tour?" he asked.

"Not yet." A castle tour was one of the suggested itinerary items listed in her information package, but Jenna had yet to book anything. She'd told Shirley it was because she wanted to be spontaneous, but really it was because she'd been too busy before departure. "I thought I'd take a day and soak in the atmosphere first."

"You should, if only to appreciate the atmosphere in which you are soaking. Did you know, for example, that the wine cellar doubled as a meeting locale for les Compagnies du Soleil during the White Terror?"

"The white what?"

"When members of the region took revenge on those who supported the revolution. That would be *our* revolution, by the way," he added. A dimple in his left cheek punctuated his cheeky grin.

"You mean they were rebelling against the rebellion?" she asked.

"We prefer to think of it as an attempt to preserve tradition. And perhaps their heads."

"No, they definitely wouldn't want to lose those." She wondered how many women had lost their heads over this guy. She'd met men like him before. Players, albeit not as suave.

Or as handsome, the voice reminded her.

Men like him were the worst, because they tricked you. Most poseurs were so obvious you knew not to take them seriously. This kind of guy, however… This was the kind of guy who sucked you in with their smoothness, leading you to believe he were sincerely interested in more than sex. Next thing you knew, you were spending your life like a puppet, dancing a jig every time he jerked your string.

This guy looked like someone who pulled a lot of strings.

He leaned an elbow against the rail, allowing his eyes to lock with Jenna's. "Speak for yourself, mademoiselle. Sometimes losing your head can be rather fun."

"Not in my experience," Jenna replied.

"Perhaps you haven't had the right experience."

If she were in Nantucket, this would be the point where she told him to take a hike. Instead, whether it was the jet lag, the champagne on an empty stomach or the heady French atmosphere, she found herself leaning into his gaze. The hue was far deeper and richer than she realized. More blue-violet than purple, making them even more unique. And captivating...

"How did they make out? The rebels against the rebellion. Did they keep their heads?" she asked him.

"You'll have to take the tour to find out." The dimple reappeared. "Unless you would like a more personal tour."

Despite knowing better, the offer went straight to the base of her spine.

"French history just happens to be a personal passion of mine," he told her. "Particularly the d'Usay family."

Wait? Was he offering her an actual tour? "Won't you get in trouble? With the hotel?" she added when he gave her a quizzical look. There was personalized service, and then there was personalized service. "I wouldn't want to take you away from the other guests."

An amused smile tugged the corner of his mouth. "I'm sure the other guests will survive."

Jenna debated the offer, turning her phone end over end as she thought. What the heck—it was only a walk around the hotel, not a marriage proposal. Besides, unlike most guys on the make, this one was actually entertaining. If he got annoying, she could always beg off by blaming jet lag. "In that case, I would love a tour."

"Wonderful. My name is Philippe, by the way."

"Jenna Brown."

"*Enchanté*, Jenna Brown."

Amazing how an accent could turn the plainest of New England names exotic and sensual. Particularly when the words were accompanied by a sweep of admiring eyes. Again, she found herself throwing out Nantucket rules. Instead of being insulted, she felt goose bumps trail in its wake.

He motioned toward the door. "Shall we?"

Jenna scooped up her wine on the way past her table. Let the adventure begin.

"An auction, you say?"

"A fund-raising auction," Jenna replied. "People bid on different experiences, each to be held at a Merchant hotel. One hundred percent of the profits went to build a clinic for recovering drug addicts on Cape Cod. Our area has a terrible opioid addiction issue."

They were descending a spiral stone staircase, having discovered the door to the western tower was locked. Philippe might have been flirting when he offered a tour, but, to her surprise, he took his tour guide duties quite seriously. Jenna found herself treated to a master class in regional history and the colorful role the d'Usay family played in it.

At some point, the conversation had turned to her, though, and now she was explaining about the inheritance that brought her to France.

"Sounds like a very noble cause," Philippe remarked.

"It is, although I have to confess that when my friend Shirley convinced me to go, helping the opioid crisis wasn't my primary motive. I went looking for adventure."

"Is that so?" He stopped midstep.

The spark in his eyes set the goose bumps skittering again. Tempted as she was to pretend otherwise—because why not pretend on vacation?—it was time to burst his bubble. In case he thought her a rich American on holiday. "The vacation," she clarified. "I'm a nurse in a nursing home back in Massachusetts. One of my patients left me an inheritance with orders that I use the money to have an adventure."

"Interesting terms for an inheritance." If he was disappointed by her lack of wealth, the re-action didn't show on his face. She'd studied closely to notice a change. His eyes remained intently focused on her.

"Not if you knew Beatrice. She was like Auntie Mame on steroids. Wore red lipstick and a silk kimono right up to the end." She smiled at the memory. "The two of us would watch travel documentaries, and she would mock me for not having seen enough of the world. 'If you're not careful, you grow old and boring,' she used to tell me."

"That doesn't sound very sweet."

"It was all in good fun. I made the mis-take of telling her I'd never been farther than

Mexico on spring break. She insisted she was going to leave the nursing home and the two of us would take one last adventure together."

Feeling a lump rising in her throat, she looked away so he wouldn't see the moisture teasing her eyes. "Adding the stipulation to the inheritance was her way of making sure one of us did."

"How fortunate for us you decided to have your adventure here."

"My friend Shirley was supposed to come, too, but unfortunately she got sick at the last minute."

"Well, if you find you need company..."

The practiced way the words came off his tongue said she wasn't the first to hear them. Didn't stop her insides from growing warm, however.

"It's okay. I'm a pro at having fun on my own."

Sidestepping the offer for the moment, she pointed to a giant portrait hanging on the wall across from the bottom step. "What can you tell me about this painting?"

The middle-aged couple in 1930s period clothing looked to be overseeing the tower traffic. There was something very striking about the portrait. The couple looked intimidating, but in a regal way. From their place on the wall, their eyes could judge everyone who went up and down the stairs.

"That is Antoinette and Simon d'Usay." Philippe stopped and leaned against the stairway's stone rail. "They were the last of the d'Usays to actually live in the castle. After World War I, they built Château d'Usay."

"On the other side of the lavender fields." Jenna had read about the smaller château, which was still three times as large as anything she'd seen, in the guidebook. Seeing it, and its rolling purple fields, was one of the trip highlights she'd most been looking forward to.

"You won't be disappointed," he replied when she told him. "Château d'Usay remains the largest producer of lavender in the region. Many of the top perfumes in the country rely on d'Usay blossoms for their scents."

There was pride in his voice. She wondered if all the locals felt this way or if he had a particular affinity for the d'Usay family because of their rich history.

She thought of her own family and its history of codependency and bad decisions. There definitely weren't residents of Somerville waxing proudly about the Brown family's contribution to society.

"So much history attached to one family," she mused. "In a way, it's a shame they decided to sell the castle."

"Buildings this age are very expensive to maintain," he replied. "Mold, rot, water damage—they take their toll. Better to let a corporation keep the building in existence rather than let it crumble from neglect like other abandoned French relics."

He had a point. Even if the castle weren't centuries old, the size alone would make upkeep a fortune. Slowly, she made her way down the rest of the staircase until she stopped in front of the painting. The couple looked familiar. A byproduct of spending weeks studying hotel literature and web guides, she'd bet. "Does the family still live in the region?"

"If you call a single person a family. There is only one direct descendent left."

"Really." She'd expected him to say that half the valley was related to them or something. Glancing over, she noticed Philippe studying the painting with a frown.

"Life hasn't been good to the d'Usays over the last decade," he said. "Only two of Simon and Antoinette's children lived to adulthood, and only one of them had children. A son, Marcel. He died in the late twentieth century."

"How sad. For a family to survive a thousand years only to fade away."

"Happens to all families, eventually." His frown sharpened momentarily, only to disappear just as quickly. Once again he was the charming flirt from the terrace. "So let us talk about more pleasant topics. Such as dinner. Would you care to join me this evening?"

So smooth. Such polish. Jenna had no doubt he would pull out all the stops and that dinner would be a romantic, seductive affair. Designed to melt her heart and inhibitions.

"There aren't rules about fraternizing with guests?" she asked, pretty sure that he wouldn't care if there were.

Sure enough. That amused smile from earlier returned to his face, and he shrugged. "I won't tell if you won't."

She met his gaze again. Dear Lord, but his eyes sucked you in. She'd bet he made every woman he met feel like the only woman in the world. Until the next woman crossed his path, that was.

"I appreciate the offer, but…" Shirley was going to kill her. "I think I'm going to stay in and order from room service tonight. Alone," she added, for extra emphasis.

He took the rejection like a pro. "Another

time, then. We can have what you Americans call a rain check."

"Sure." Like that would happen. "Thank you for the tour."

"It was my pleasure." She gasped as he caught her hand and raised it to his lips. "*Au revoir*, Jenna Brown," he said, planting a soft kiss on her knuckles. "I look forward to our paths crossing again."

"*Au revoir,*" Jenna replied. She stood on the stairs and watched as he strolled away in search of someone else to charm. The first, and likely the only, sexy Frenchman of the trip.

Oh well, she thought, rubbing her knuckles, *easy come, easy go*.

Philippe waited until the American disappeared around the corner before heading to the front desk. The petite brown-haired woman—girl, really—straightened with recognition. "Is there something I can do for you?" she asked. Philippe didn't miss the eagerness sparkling in her eyes, or the way she flipped her hair over her shoulder when she spoke.

"*Oui,*" he replied. "I was wondering if you might do me a favor… The American, Mademoiselle Brown…"

"Whatever he asks, Nicole, the answer is no."

Yves St. Dumond, the hotel manager, suddenly appeared in the office doorway. A large man with thickset features and silver hair, he placed a beefy hand on Nicole's shoulder. "This hotel is not your personal playground, Philippe. If you want to pick up women, go someplace else."

"I'm hurt." Philippe pressed a hand to his chest. "Haven't you known me long enough to know that if I wanted to seduce a guest, I wouldn't need to bother your staff?" To prove a point, he winked at Nicole, who, on cue, blushed.

"Then what is it you need?"

A distraction. Something—or someone—to keep him from falling into a week-long dark hole.

"It's August," he replied.

Yves's expression immediately softened. "*Je suis désolé*. I wasn't thinking. I lost track of the date."

"So did I. Almost." In the end, the calendar reminded him, like it always did.

The consistency was almost humorous. Every year he vowed that this would be the year he broke the pattern, but apparently he was a glutton for punishment, because he insisted on returning for harvest every year. How could he not? Harvest remained a tradition in his family—even if he was a family of one. It was the least he could do for his family. His penance for being the last of the d'Usays.

He forced a smile. "Don't worry. I'll be out of your hair soon enough." He just had to survive a few weeks. Come September, the yearning for whatever it was he yearned for would cease and he'd return to his apartment in Arles.

"In the meantime, why are you interested in Mademoiselle Brown? She's certainly not your usual type."

"No, she is not." Philippe preferred shallow women who had expensive tastes and short attention spans. Women like him. Jenna Brown with her copper hair and shorts with tiny whales was as far from his type as he could imagine.

Perhaps that was why he'd noticed her the moment he stepped onto the hotel terrace. Sitting there, getting frustrated with her inability to take a self-portrait. He found that particular lack of skill extremely attractive.

Add what was obviously a sharp mind and dry wit… Yes, she was exactly the distraction he needed. "Nevertheless, I found her very stimulating and would enjoy spending more time with her."

"Meaning you've already spent time with her. Why didn't you simply ask her to dinner? Wait a moment…" Yves's eyes widened. "Don't tell me she turned you down."

"I believe it is called a rain check," Philippe replied.

Something else that stirred his interest. There had been obvious attraction in her green eyes, and yet she'd still said no. He couldn't remember the last time a woman rebuffed his advances. What his looks didn't accomplish, his name usually did.

And there was what might be the most attractive thing of all about Mademoiselle Brown: she had no clue as to who he was. Their interaction had been based solely on his charm and her interest in their conversation. He found it amazingly refreshing.

"Which brings me back to why I need Nicole's assistance," he said. "She's going to help me cash in my rain check."

A frisson of anticipation passed through him. He couldn't wait to see Jenna Brown's face when their paths crossed again.

CHAPTER TWO

JENNA HAD A HEADACHE. Too much sun and strong floral aroma had left a knot behind her eyes. She needed a glass of water and some pain relievers. Hopefully the word *aspirin* was the same in French?

Day two of her adventure wasn't off to a very auspicious start.

She never did eat dinner. She'd fallen into a deep sleep shortly after she returned to her room and woke up before dawn starved and eager to start her adventure. Since Philippe had sounded so enthusiastic about the excursion to Château d'Usay, she took his advice and signed up. Part of her wondered if she'd see him at the front desk when she went downstairs, but the only person she saw was a sweet girl named Nicole who grinned every time Jenna gave her name. She wondered if Philippe had found a dinner companion after they parted ways? Immediately, she pictured a leggy French heiress and felt a prick of annoyance in her stomach. More because she was thinking about Philippe than because of the woman she imagined. It wasn't like her to dwell on a random stranger. Philippe with his mesmerizing eyes should be no exception.

She had to give him props, though. The tour was as interesting as he'd promised. They began in the greenhouse, where she and other visitors learned about the various varieties and uses for lavender. The d'Usays, they were told, grew *lavande fine*, or "true" lavender rather than the more popular *lavandin*.

"The *lavandin* actually produces more oil per flower," the guide told them. "The family has a separate property a few kilometers away, which provides the bulk of their harvest. Here at Château d'Usay, however, they continue to grow *lavande fine* as they always have."

The family certainly liked to maintain its tradition, didn't it? Jenna crouched to take a picture of the spiny purple flower up close. The deep purple blossoms reminded her of Philippe's eyes.

After a visit to the fields, where they were given a lesson on Provençal climate and agriculture, as well as ample photo opportunities, their group made their way across a limestone pavilion to the château itself, the final stop before they visited the lavender store. It was in the fields that the knot had morphed into a full-blown headache. Making matters worse, today's tour guide had a high-pitched voice that turned into a high pitched squeak whenever she feigned enthusiasm. She must have chirped the phrase, "In the world!" at least a dozen times, her voice piping upward each time.

The group made their way up the front steps, where they found themselves in a large marble entranceway dominated by a large staircase. Several audible sighs could be heard as the temperature dropped several degrees.

Their guide pointed to a portrait guarding the entrance. Simon and Antoinette d'Usay, captured many years after the painting in the castle. Although both had gray hair and were noticeably heavier, their eyes were still sharp and intimidating. "This is Simon and Antoinette d'Usay, who built the château after the First World War. It's considered one of the finest examples of French Renaissance Revival architecture in the world. I'm sorry, sir, the staircase is off-limits."

She was talking to one of the older tourists, who had moved too close to the velvet rope blocking the stairs. "Those lead to the family's private rooms."

"Does the Comte d'Usay still live here?" someone asked.

"We do not use titles in France. They were eliminated with the revolution. To answer your question, however, Monsieur d'Usay lives most of the year in Arles. Although he does visit from time to time. Now, follow me through these doors. The next room we'll see is the main salon, or as the family called it, *le Salon des Fleurs.*"

Jenna hung in the back of the line as the guide led the group through the double doors. No way she was going to handle that voice for the entire tour without taking an aspirin. There had to be something for sale at the store. Surely, she wasn't the only person to take the tour and suffer from lavender overload.

Her sandals made a tiny squeaking noise on the tile as she turned around.

"Running away, Mademoiselle Brown?" a familiar voice asked.

Philippe? Her ears had to be playing tricks on her. Why would he be touring the mansion? When she looked to her left, however, there he was. Walking down the stairs in a pair of faded jeans and a white linen shirt that gaped ever so nicely. As opposed to her mouth, which simply gaped. *What on earth?*

He grinned, the dimple in full bloom. "Didn't I tell you our paths would cross again?"

"Yes, but how did…?" *Wait a second.* Jenna rewound her thoughts. He was coming *down the stairs. Where the family stayed.*

"No way," she said. "You can't be…"

"Can't be what?" Stepping off the bottom step, he sidestepped the velvet barrier to join her at the room's center. "You aren't wearing your little whales today," he said.

Took her a moment to realize he was referring to her shorts. After noting yesterday that none of the other women at the resort wore shorts, she'd ditched them in favor of a Lilly Pulitzer shift and platform sandals. The pink tropical print still marked her as an American tourist, but at least she was slightly more stylish.

"No," she replied.

"You look lovely."

"Thank you. What were you doing upstairs?"

"What do you think?"

"You work here?" But even as she asked, she knew the answer. He was dressed too casually, and his eyes sparkled too brightly for an employee.

"How could I possible work here and at the hotel?" he asked before leaning in and adding, "That is what you thought yesterday, is it not?"

"You were wearing a hotel uniform."

"Was I?"

Yes. The same dark suit as the concierge and desk manager. Granted, his was more finely tailored, and he hadn't been wearing a name tag, but…

She looked over her shoulder at the portrait on the wall, before looking back to Philippe. He bore the same regal carriage as Simon and Antoinette.

"Philippe d'Usay, at your service." He swept his arm wide and bowed. "Welcome to Château d'Usay."

Shoot. Her. Now. "Why didn't you say anything? If I'd known, I would never have…"

"Been such relaxed and enjoyable company?" he supplied. "Precisely why I didn't correct your mistake. You have to understand, everyone in Avignon knows who I am. I found it refreshing to meet someone who did not."

How nice for him that she could be a novelty. She wasn't sure what was worse—her mistaking him for an employee or his deception. "Must have been very entertaining, having to give me that tour."

"It was."

And what if she'd said yes to his dinner invitation? How long would he have carried on the masquerade? Through the meal? Later? "Well, bully for you."

"Jenna, wait. I'm not explaining myself well. You think I was playing a game."

"Weren't you?" Her eyes traveled to where he'd caught her hand as she tried to turn away. The gold signet ring on his little finger gleamed against his tanned skin. Ten to one that was a d'Usay family crest engraved on it. She felt like such an idiot.

"Not the way you think. I did not intentionally mean to mislead you."

Jenna raised a brow.

"All right, it was intentional, but it wasn't malicious. I told you, everyone in the valley knows who I am. When I realized you didn't recognize me, it was a chance for me to be simply Philippe, without all the baggage that comes with being a d'Usay."

Sure, and Jenna had a Roman bridge she wanted to sell him. The man wasn't even trying to look apologetic. His eyes twinkled with amusement.

"You don't really expect me to believe that line, do you?" she asked.

The dimples appeared. "It was worth a shot."

Of all the… She should be annoyed by the deception. She should be insulted. In fact, she should be a lot of things. Smiling was not one of them. But darn if she couldn't help catching his good humor.

"Didn't anyone ever tell you it's not nice to lie?" she said.

"Would you have believed me if I told the truth?"

That he used to own the castle? No, she would have told him to get lost, because no one owned castles.

"I rest my case," he said after she answered. "And then you and I would not have had the opportunity to spend time together. So in the end, my lie of omission was a good thing."

"I'm not sure I'd use the word *good*," Jenna replied. It was meant to be a grumble, but the corners of her mouth insisted on curving upward.

"But not entirely bad, either, no?"

Much as she hated to admit it, he was right. "No, not entirely bad."

"*Merci, ma chère.*" He smiled down through his lashes, the purple a dash darker than before.

That's when Jenna realized they were still

holding hands. Lightly, but Philippe's grip had enough firmness to cause a flutter of awareness. Warmth spread to her cheeks.

"Could I…?" She dropped her gaze down to their hands.

"But of course." He released her, stuffing his hands into his back pockets. Her palm suddenly feeling naked, Jenna had to settle for running a hand over the back of her hair.

"Now, tell me," he said. "What is it that has you running out of my house in the middle of your tour?"

Her headache. In her surprise, she'd nearly forgotten the reason she was sneaking away from the tour in the first place. "I wasn't running," she told him. "I was heading to the gift shop in search of water and aspirin. No offense, but your lavender gave me a headache."

"None taken," he replied. "The aroma can be overpowering if you are not used to it. But there's no need to go all the way to the gift shop. Come with me."

"Where are we going?" She glanced over her shoulder. Philippe was guiding her past the stairs to a corridor, the end of which was also blocked by a velvet rope.

"To the kitchen to get you a glass of water," he said.

"But…my tour."

"Will carry on without you," he said. "I will make sure you meet up with them in time to return to the hotel."

She glanced over her shoulder. The group must have moved to another room; she could no longer hear the guide's chirp. "Aspirin and water. No more."

"Absolutely, *ma chère*," he replied. "You have my word."

Said the man who'd already misled her once. Apparently Jenna had left her common sense in America, because she followed him anyway.

The kitchen was out of a French countryside fantasy. Big and airy, with an abundance of copper pots and pans. There was a battered butcher-block table and gleaming stainless steel appliances. The stove alone, Jenna decided, would eat up her entire kitchen back home.

The air smelled of fresh bread and lemons. A wonderful change from the floral notes she'd been breathing all morning. "Were you baking?" she asked.

"That would be the *fougasse*. My housekeeper, Henrietta, makes a point of baking it whenever I visit the house. Would you care for some?"

"Depends. What is it?"

"Only a slice of heaven wrapped in a golden crust," he said with a laugh. "Sit down and I will get you your aspirin. Henrietta keeps a bottle in the cupboard."

Jenna did as she was told, settling herself on the bench while Philippe opened and closed cabinet doors. A part of her still couldn't quite believe he owned the château, despite his obvious comfort with the surroundings.

"Do you come here often?" she asked. The corniness of her question struck her, and she nearly rolled her eyes at her own lameness. "I meant the house. The guide mentioned that you don't live here full-time."

"She is correct. I have an apartment in Arles, near our executive offices."

"I'm surprised."

"Success! It was with the spices." He held up a bottle of white tablets. Taking the bottle, Jenna saw the label read *aspirine*.

"Why are you surprised?" he asked.

"Considering how poetic you were about the countryside yesterday, I would have thought you'd spend as much time here as possible."

"I also appreciate a fine Beaujolais, but I would get bored drinking it every evening. I much prefer the variety of the city. One can only sit around and listen to the drone of the bees for so long."

He returned with a glass of ice water and an earthenware platter on which Jenna saw a flatbread sculpted to look like an ear of wheat. Sitting next to her, he immediately tore off a chunk and offered it to her. "I promise, you will not be disappointed."

"And if I am?"

"Then you have no soul."

Jenna tasted the bread. The warm crust broke away to reveal a soft inside that tasted of rosemary and orange.

"See? I told you," he said, tearing off a piece for himself. "No one makes *fougasse* like Henrietta."

For a few moments, they ate in silence. Whether it was the aspirin or the change in aromas or both, Jenna could feel her headache receding. Food helped, too, just as Philippe suggested. Every so often she stole a look sideways to watch him. He didn't eat the bread; he experienced it. His eyes would close and a contented smile would curl his lips upward as he savored each bite. The sight was almost as pleasurable as tasting the bread.

A thought struck her. "Why were you certain we'd see each other again? When you were on the stairs, you said you knew we'd meet again."

He was in mid-savor when she asked her question, so he pried open one eye. "What can I say? I believe in fate. And…" A hint of pink crept into his cheeks. "I may have asked the front desk to call me when you signed up for the hotel excursion."

"What?" No wonder the girl at the desk kept smiling at her. She was in on the joke.

"I did not want to take a chance on missing your visit. Tours come and go all day long."

"So you asked for advance information."

"I prefer to think of it as arranging for fate to be on my side."

Jenna narrowed her eyes. "You could have called my room and asked me."

"But that would have spoiled the surprise. And you were surprised, no?"

"Hmm." She continued to stare at him with narrowed eyes. Honest to God, she'd never heard of someone doing such a thing. Asking a clerk to tip him off. Certainly no one interested in her had ever gone to such lengths. "You're incorrigible. You know that, right?"

"Oui."

He leaned closer, the gap in his shirt treating her to a glimpse of the smooth skin beneath. "And you are flattered. I can see it in your eyes."

Jenna was flattered—immensely—but she wasn't about to let him know. "How do you know it's not amusement at your arrogance?"

"Amusement doesn't make a woman's skin flush."

Flashing a smug smile, he sat back in his chair. "I am sorry about your headache. That was not part of my plan. Is it better?"

"Getting there."

"Good. I'm glad. I forget how pungent the smell of lavender can be. When we were children, my brother Felix and I complained incessantly about the aroma." While speaking, he reached for her glass. The ice clinked as he lifted it high for a drink.

"You have a brother? Yesterday on the tour you said you were…" Jenna paused.

"The last of the line? I am. My brother died of cancer several years ago."

He spoke with nonchalance, but Jenna caught a shadow in his eyes as he raised the glass to his lips for another drink.

"I'm sorry."

"So am I. He was a good man." He fell silent for a moment as a shadow darkened his features. Only for a moment, though. Jenna would have missed it altogether had she not been watching closely. "Let us talk about something more pleasant, shall we?"

He'd made a similar request yesterday. It was obvious he didn't like dwelling on his family. "What would you like to talk about?" she asked.

"How about dinner? Clearly, since fate has reunited us, we are destined to enjoy a meal together."

"You mean fate and a front desk clerk."

"A technicality. I knew we were destined to share each other's company as soon as I saw you on the terrace."

He was smooth. Charming, too. Much as she hated to admit it, Jenna enjoyed his company. He kept her on her toes. Dinner could be fun, as long as she kept her wits about her.

"Well, a girl does have to eat," she told him. "I might as well have some company."

He grinned like he'd won the lottery. "*Ma chère*, a woman needs to do more than eat. You need to experience French cuisine. Tonight, I shall make sure you have an experience you'll never forget."

"We'll see about that," Jenna replied. "I don't impress easily."

"Is that so? In that case..." He leaned in

again, the purple in his eyes taking on a dangerously mischievous glint that made Jenna's insides flutter in spite of herself. "I look forward to meeting your challenge."

You know I was kidding about having a fling, right? All I meant was don't be your usual picky self.

I'm not having a fling; I'm having dinner.

Despite what Philippe d'Usay might think, her "French experience" was beginning and ending with dinner.

I don't do flings, remember?

You don't do anything.

That's not true. I do plenty.

Since when?

Since...

Jenna paused before hitting the backspace button. So it had been a while. Big deal. She was taking a dating hiatus. All the sweet talk and pretend interest in commitment that ended after a few weeks? Who needed it. She was trying to break her family pattern, not contribute to it.

Excuse me for being selective.

She leaned back against the headboard. Shirley's thoughts didn't need a phone for her to hear them. Her friend had given her the tough-love speech a half dozen times over the past couple years. *You're too picky. You never give anyone a chance. You rule guys out before you ever get a chance to know them.*

Maybe, Jenna thought, she was picky because she wanted more than a guy who claimed to want a relationship only to bail when he got bored. Of all people, Shirley should understand why.

Her phone buzzed. Shirley had replied.

This guy must be something if you are giving him the time of day.

He's okay.

Actually, he was everything Jenna claimed to detest. A guy like Philippe wasn't interested in depth. She wondered if he even knew what the word meant. And yet as bad an idea as the man was, he intrigued her in a way she hadn't felt in a long, long time.

After their conversation in the kitchen, Philippe had walked her through his back garden to the gift shop.

"Until tonight," he'd said, kissing her hand. Affected as all get-out, it still managed to set her entire arm aflame. The entire bus ride home, she found herself reliving the moment. If a kiss to the hand could set off her inner fireworks, she'd wondered, what would a real kiss do? Or...?

Her phone buzzed.

Just okay?

Maybe a little more than okay.

If her friend could only see him.

In that case, you know what they say. What happens in France...

Ha-ha.

All I'm saying is keep an open mind. A little fun

never hurt anyone. Remember, Beatrice wanted you to have an adventure.

Somehow she didn't think Beatrice meant falling into bed with a sexy stranger.

Since when are you so invested in my sex life, anyway?

Since I'm home with shingles and no one wants to come near me. One of us ought to have a good time.

Jenna shook her head.

Sorry, babe. You're simply going to have to use your imagination.

Killjoy.

Yep. I've got to go get ready. TTYL.

She exited the application before Shirley could respond with Do what I'd do or some other nonsensical words of encouragement.

Tossing the phone on the bed beside her, Jenna stared at the black silk dress currently hanging on the door of her armoire. It was a simple wrap dress, modest by most standards. It was also the only fancy item she'd packed, since she hadn't actually planned on any dating or dining alone in super-fancy restaurants. Was it fancy enough for wherever Philippe intended to take her? He'd said he'd pick her up at eight, but he hadn't said where they were going.

All of a sudden, Jenna felt nervous. She was being silly. What did she care whether her wardrobe was appropriate? Wasn't as though any of the people in the restaurant would see her again. And it wasn't as if she was trying to impress Philippe. Then again, she didn't want to embarrass herself, either.

"Clothes, schmothes," Beatrice had said once. "Like anyone cares." At the time, she'd been insisting on wearing her silk robe—just her silk robe—to the dining room. "I'll have you know I ate naked once when I was in Bali."

Good old Beatrice, feisty and independent until the end. She didn't care what people thought. Married thirty years to her partner in crime, she'd told Jenna. Until he wasn't a partner anymore. Then she moved on. "No sense wasting your time on something that's not working," she'd said. What she would think of Philippe, Jenna could only imagine.

Never trust a man who's prettier than you,

she immediately thought in Beatrice's raspy voice.

It was a good rule. Especially since Philippe was prettier than everyone.

Philippe entered the hotel early. Usually he didn't pay attention to time, as the women he called on always kept him waiting. Instinct told him Jenna was the kind of woman who appreciated promptness. He chose not to think about the fact that he'd spent the last thirty minutes dressed and watching the clock.

He smoothed the front of his dinner jacket. Funny, but he was actually anxious about the evening going well. He'd spent the entire afternoon planning the perfect dinner, which was one afternoon more than he'd spent planning any of his previous dates. Why bother when a table at the hottest club or restaurant would suffice? Tonight, however, required more. Mademoiselle Brown had a cynical streak, meaning she wouldn't be easily impressed. That required he put an effort into the evening.

Which was good. Planning kept him from brooding, and he despised brooding. There was nothing he could do about the tragedies life dealt him. He hated that he was forever dodging a shadow of sadness. It was far better to distract oneself with living.

Or a beautiful woman.

Simon and Antoinette greeted him on his way to the elevator. He stopped to say hello, as he always did when visiting. They greeted him with their usual haughty stares.

Did his ancestors approve of how he was running their empire? He'd like to think he was doing a good job, but he was also aware that he was never meant to be the one running D'Usay International. Felix was the one who'd been groomed to walk in their father's footsteps, and they both left very large shoes. Philippe did the best he could, but there were times when he wondered if they would approve of the changes he'd made. The expansion. The move beyond French flowers. Were they staring down in disdain or relieved their empire would continue even when the company no longer had a d'Usay in charge?

He supposed he wouldn't know until it was all over for him.

And there he went, thinking maudlin thoughts when he had a beautiful woman waiting upstairs.

Considering what Jenna had worn on their previous two meetings, he expected to see her wearing something bright and touristy. The woman who opened the door, however, was gloriously sophisticated. His eyes skimmed her length appreciatively. The black cocktail dress was classically elegant, modest but revealing in all the right places. Arousal curled through him. *"Tu es belle."*

She smiled appreciatively. "I'm going to assume it was a compliment."

"It was. I said you look beautiful."

To her credit, she took the compliment in stride, without the faux modesty he'd come to expect from his dates. "Thank you."

"No, thank *you*." He held out his arm. "Shall we?"

"Where are we going?"

So suspicious. He would definitely need to work if he wanted tonight to end successfully. The challenge was exactly what he needed.

He patted her hand. "Wait and see, Mademoiselle Brown," he replied. "I promise you will not be disappointed."

CHAPTER THREE

"IS ALL THIS for us?"

Philippe swelled with satisfaction as he watched Jenna walk across the terrace. Her reaction was everything he'd hoped for and more. He watched as she circled the candlelit table with wide-eyed astonishment.

"Would you prefer a table on the main terrace?" He had requested a private table on the northeast terrace overlooking the garden. The cloudless night was perfect for dining outside, the full moon and lanterns casting a silvery light over everything.

"This is… I mean, I wasn't expecting…" She paused her exploration to look up at him. "You shouldn't have gone to all this trouble," she said.

"You said this was a fantasy vacation. I figured why not give you a fantastical dinner?"

"Fantastical dinner?" she repeated.

Even from a distance, Philippe could see the wariness in her eyes. Questioning his expectations. And why shouldn't she? His intentions were fairly obvious. Also obvious was that Jenna Brown wasn't a woman easily swept off her feet. But then, he'd suspected as much, which was why he'd gone to all this effort.

Apparently his work wasn't finished.

"An experience that would make your late friend proud," he replied. "And your texting friend jealous."

"Mission accomplished. On both points. This is…" She swung her arm around. "Wow."

"You approve. I'm glad."

He watched as she moved to the terrace rail, her skirt flowing around her knees. Most of his dates preferred to bare as much flesh as possible. Miles of it, actually, all toned and tanned to perfection. He never would have guessed how erotic—and arousing—pale modesty could be.

"The garden looks beautiful from here," she said. "You don't get an appreciation of the layout when you're on ground level."

He joined her. Normally, he would take advantage of the moment to encircle her waist from behind. Instead, he stood to her left, his hand resting on the railing a millimeter from hers. Below them, the garden spread out in perfect geometric symmetry. Concentric squares marked in the center by a giant fountain. The stone paths that bordered each square looked whiter than usual thanks to a series of strategically placed spotlights.

"French gardens are designed to be enjoyed both up close and from a distance. So that when people look down from their upper stories, they will experience the garden's beauty as a whole."

"Do you think your ancestors stood here once upon a time, or is this part of the newer construction?" she asked, leaning forward.

"They might have." He was fibbing slightly. The private terraces *were* part of the new construction, but the room leading to them was original, and she sounded too enchanted to disappoint.

And her eyes… He took in her profile, admiring how the green sparkled in the moonlight. "The garden was designed to resemble the original as closely as possible."

"Really?" She turned, and Philippe sucked in his breath when confronted with the fullness of her wide-eyed wonder. The woman respected tradition. Bravo to her.

"I provided the photographs," he told her.

"It's gorgeous. This is the first time I've seen the fountain under lights. I wanted to explore last night, but I was too jet-lagged to do anything, including eat."

"Should I worry about you falling asleep during dinner?"

"That depends," she said.

"On?"

She grinned. "How entertaining you are during the meal."

Challenge accepted. "Do not worry. I can be very entertaining." The muscles in his hand twitched as he fought the urge to mark a trail along her arm. Too forward, and he would scare her off.

That didn't mean he couldn't let his eyes complete the innuendo. Her eyes responded in kind, the pupils growing wide. He watched as she swallowed away the rest of her physical response. Rather, she tried to. It remained in the depths of her gaze. The air between them pulsed. Once. Twice.

Jenna broke the silence. "What is that scent?" she asked. "It's not lavender."

"Jasmine," he answered. "The aroma is stronger in the evenings. Do you see those white flowers?"

Reluctantly, he raised his arm—taking it away

from the warmth of her proximity—to point out the bushes lining one of the inner squares. "Our Grasse property has a large jasmine crop. We'll harvest the blossoms in a few weeks and sell them to the perfumeries for use in their fragrances."

She nodded as though digesting a great truth. "Would it be sacrilegious if I said I like the scent more than lavender?" she asked him.

"Only if you say the words loudly." No surprise, given her headache earlier. Jasmine had a far lighter scent.

Light scents would definitely suit her more, he decided. As surreptitiously as possible, he leaned to inhale the air near the crook of her neck. Notes of citrus caught his nostrils. Clean and crisp.

"You don't wear perfume," he noted. A foreign concept in his world.

"Got out of the habit, I'm afraid. Strong smells sometimes bother my patients, so I find it easier to avoid them altogether."

"Shame. I'm of the belief that a woman should always wear perfume. The right scent can transform a woman from ordinary to something mysterious and seductive that is indelible to the mind. Eye color, the curve of her cheek—those may fade from memory, but the smell of her perfume? That is something the brain never forgets."

"Says the man who makes his money selling flowers to perfume companies."

She had him there. "Perhaps I am a tad biased."

"Just a tad," she said with a sideways glance.

It was the perfect night for dining outside. The trill of a piano floated in on the breeze to join the crickets in a summer duet. Philippe absorbed the sound as he took in Jenna's profile. "What is it?" he asked when a smile broke across her features.

"Nothing." The pink that immediately filled her cheeks was adorable. "I was looking at the garden and it dawned on me that you're a farmer. That's harder to imagine than you working for the hotel."

"You can't picture me digging in the dirt?"

"In a word? No."

Philippe laughed. "Don't worry. Neither can I. For the sake of everyone involved, I leave the actual agriculture to those with far greener thumbs. Otherwise we run the risk of destroying half the region."

"Surely you don't have that black a thumb."

"Don't be so sure. My brother, Felix, once made me swear that I would never interfere with that side of the business. He didn't appreciate how I managed to kill a lemon tree he'd bought me."

Your apartment is where plants go to die was what he'd actually said. Nearly set off his vital monitor for laughing, too. His nurse scowled at them for being rambunctious.

"I take it he…"

"Had a green thumb?" he asked, to save her from stumbling over tense. "Very much so. He loved the farms, especially the lavender fields. He'd come out every summer to help with the harvests. He lived for this time of year."

"What about you? Do you live for this time of year as well?"

Did he live for a season that reminded him of the family he lost? An honest answer would kill the moment. Now was not the time to think of life's injustices. Not when there was champagne chilling and a beautiful woman to share it with. "Come," he said, taking her hand. "Before the champagne grows flat."

The bottle sat in a silver ice bucket waiting to be poured. While they'd been talking, he'd heard the *pop!* as a waiter carefully uncorked the bottle and then disappeared. Philippe filled the glasses and handed one to Jenna. "To bucket lists and fantastical memories," he said before washing away his less fantastical ones.

"I killed an air fern once."

He coughed as the last swallow caught in his throat. "*Pardon*?"

"It's a plant that only needs watering every couple weeks. Very low maintenance. I killed it. I also killed a terrarium. And I'm pretty sure I'm the reason my poinsettia bit the dust last Christmas as well. To this day I cringe when one of my patients offers me a plant. Might as well just give the thing a death sentence and be done with it."

Her effort to lighten the mood succeeded. The shadow retreated farther. "So you're saying we're both horticulturally challenged?"

"I was going to say we're plant angels of death, but your phrase sounds better."

Indeed. But hers made him smile. Doubly so, because he suspected she was being outrageous for his sake. "A second toast then," he said. "To sparing nature from our deadly touch."

"To giving plants a fighting chance," she replied.

Philippe clinked his glass to hers and downed the contents. "So Jenna Brown saves lives and kills plants. What else does she do?"

"Do?"

"Tell me about yourself." To his surprise he was genuinely interested in her answer. "Your family. Do they live in Nantucket as well?"

"No. They're in Boston."

There was tightness in her voice. He'd touched a nerve. "I'm sorry. It is an unpleasant subject."

"Yes and no," she replied with a sigh. "My parents... Let's just say they have a complicated relationship and leave it at that."

Very well. He knew when not to push. "And your job? You enjoy being a nurse in...?" Where was it she told him she worked? "A nursing home?"

A switch flipped inside her. "Absolutely. I love my patients. Some of them are like family."

A family that eventually died on her. While her living family was estranged. Philippe didn't understand. "It doesn't bother you, spending all your time around death?" He marveled at her answer. How could anyone love watching people die?

"Death is a part of life. I'm glad I can be there at the end to help them leave this world with dignity."

No, Philippe thought, death was a thief, taking good people before their time. "All the more reason to pack as much life as possible into our time on earth. Since death is inevitable."

"You sound very French."

"I'm only quoting you, and we are a fatalistic people."

"Is that what you are?"

"Hardly," he replied. "I'm much more of a hedonist."

"Pleasure above things?"

"Why not? Good wine. Beautiful women." He met her eyes as he said the last part, earning a small blush. "Life should be embraced with both hands, should it not?"

"Beatrice used to say stuff like that."

"The woman who left you the money."

Her smile softened. "She would have liked you. I remember one night we were watching a documentary about some ancient Greek city known for excessive living…"

"Sybaris," he interrupted.

She looked at him in surprise. "Yes, that's the one."

"A lucky guess. I remember the lecture from university."

"You have a very good memory."

"It was a very interesting subject," he said with a shrug.

"Anyway, when the show ended, Beatrice looked at me and said, 'Those Greeks had the right idea.'"

"My kind of woman."

"She must have dozed off during the part where the city was destroyed."

"Yes, but at least they enjoyed themselves on the way out." Reaching for the champagne, he filled both their glasses. "*Vie amoureuse*, as they say."

"She definitely would have liked you."

"Of course. I am a very likable person. You do not agree?" he asked at her enigmatic smile.

"Oh, I agree." He watched while she traced the rim of her glass. "You're extremely likable."

"And you find that a problem." A statement, not a question. He'd begun to notice a pattern with his American. Whenever she began to relax and enjoy herself, the wariness would rear its head to cool the enjoyment off. Such as now. Instead of laughing at his silly joke, she responded seriously.

"You do not trust me." Again, he presented the words as fact.

"You're a millionaire," she countered. "Where I come from, millionaires don't usually take women like me out to dinner."

"They don't believe in dating beautiful women?"

"They don't pull out all the stops unless they have an agenda."

Before he could reply, they were interrupted by a service. "*Pissaladière*," the man announced before lifting the cover to reveal an onion tart, crust browned to perfection.

"I hope you don't mind," he said, "but I took the liberty of selecting the menu. Various Provençal dishes I think you would enjoy."

"Case in point," she replied.

"If your point is that I am trying to impress you, then I plead guilty as charged."

"Impress me with the goal of coming back to my room."

"Again guilty." Did she expect him to deny human nature? Most women he knew would be swept off their feet by a moonlight dinner. Half of them would be in his arms before the tart arrived. With her, his efforts brought suspicion, despite his openness. It was almost as if she were afraid to enjoy herself.

He would need to rethink his approach.

"You always have the power to say no," he reminded her.

"So long as we both realize that." She smiled as she replied, but her eyes were serious.

"*Ma chère*, I never go anywhere I'm not invited. Although I hope you will save your rejection until after the tart."

He placed a slice on her plate and waited while she took a bite. When her eyes closed, he knew he'd scored his first point. No one could resist well-done French cuisine.

"Amazing," she replied.

"And that is only the beginning. By the time tonight is over, you'll have discovered that most things in Provence are amazing. And irresistible."

Philippe was right about the food. By the time dessert rolled around—melon pastry drizzled with lavender honey—Jenna was in love with French cooking. That included the French champagne. Philippe insisted on keeping both their glasses full at all times.

She wasn't stupid; she knew what he was doing. But everything tasted so amazing. With every bite—and sip—her guard slipped a little more. Before she knew it, she had literally kicked off her shoes and was enjoying herself.

They kept their dinner conversation light. He talked of Paris and local attractions. She told stories about Beatrice and some of her more colorful patients. By mutual agreement, they both avoided probing personal questions. Jenna would have liked to ask more about his brother. It was in those rare moments of personal revelation that she thought there might be more to him than mere charm. Asking questions, however, only opened the door to him asking more questions about her family. A topic best left unmentioned. Since nothing killed an evening faster than dysfunctional drama.

Sometimes there was something to be said for staying superficial.

The rattle of ice broke her thoughts. Philippe was pouring the last of the champagne into her glass. "Whoa there, cowboy. I don't think I should have any more." Her inhibitions had slipped enough.

"If you're certain."

"What, no insistence?"

"Not from me. I prefer my invitations be delivered with a clear head."

Spoken with the confidence of a man who had never wanted for an invitation. She shifted in her seat. "Thank you for dinner. It was delicious."

"You speak as if the evening is over."

Maybe because now was a good time for it to end. "It's getting late," she said.

"Nonsense, the night is young. I thought we might walk off dinner in the garden."

"And then what?"

"Then I will walk you to your door. I have no expectations, Jenna."

Bull. He had expectations; he was just telling her the final decision was up to her. Still, maybe it was the champagne getting to her, but a moonlight stroll amid the jasmine did sound lovely.

"You'll have to give me a moment to put on my shoes," she told him. "I kicked them off around the second course."

Before she could blink, he was on his knees with her discarded heels in his hand. "Allow me."

Gently cupping her heel, he guided her foot into her shoe. "We wouldn't want the crushed gravel hurting your feet," he said as he slipped the heel strap in place. His fingertips lingered a moment on the back of her ankle before he switched his attention to her other foot. This time, his fingers brushed upward ever so slightly. The sensation traveled the length of her leg. He gazed upward, and even through lowered lashes, Jenna could see the heat in his eyes.

"Now you are ready to walk."

* * *

They walked slowly and separately along the gravel paths. The air smelled sweeter in the garden. It was warmer, too. In fact, now that they were on the ground, everything seemed more. The moonlight. The soft ripple of the fountain. Jenna swore could even feel the brush of the air on her skin every time Philippe's arm moved. Without lifting a finger, he somehow managed to feel impossible close.

Then again, he *had* lifted a finger when they were on the terrace. If she concentrated, she could still feel his hands on the back of her ankle.

Philippe pointed to a line of bushes closest to the fountain. "There's your jasmine," he said. While the petals on other flowers in the garden had folded closed for the night, the jasmine's tiny white blossoms were open wide. "They bloom at night," Philippe told her. "There's a horticultural reason for it, but I won't bore you. Better to simply enjoy them as they are."

Tonight, Jenna had to agree. Plucking a flower from its stem, she twirled the blossom between her fingers and imagined the subtle scent drifting upward. Maybe she'd go back to wearing perfume after all. Then when she wanted to remember this trip, she need only inhale.

"You said you grow these in Grasse?" she asked.

"We grow everything in Grasse," he replied. "Roses in the spring. Jasmine and lavender in the summer. You can tell the time of year by how the air smells."

He lifted her hand to smell the flower she was holding, touching her for the first time since the walk began. "Jasmine suits you," he said.

"What makes you say that?"

"Because it is sweet but subtle. Rose is too floral and lavender too heavy. Jasmine, however, entices without overpowering. It doesn't need to advertise its beauty. Rather, it is perfect in its simplicity."

"Are you saying I'm simple?"

"*Ma chère*, you are far from simple. But you are perfect. And enticing."

While he was speaking, he slipped the flower from her and traced it along her cheek. Jenna's eyes fluttered shut. "You're trying to seduce me," she whispered.

The blossom brushed her lower lip. "Is it working?"

More than it should, and it frightened her.

Opening her eyes, she found herself staring into his, their color darkened to fine wine by the night sky. So dark she could almost imagine the light reflecting in them was from the stars. It left her feeling off balance.

Intoxicated.

"Philippe…"

"Shh." He pressed the flower to her lips. "Don't say no. Not yet."

Jenna didn't want to say no. That was the problem. What she wanted was for Philippe to kiss her until she couldn't breathe. The moment was right there. All she needed to do was whisper one word, and he would sweep her away.

Only to wake up in the morning hating herself. Try as she might, she couldn't do it. As magical as the moment felt, it was all surface magic, designed to seduce. She'd grown up witnessing the damage romantic illusion could do. She saw how a few well-played promises could lure a woman into believing they meant more. No matter how badly she was tempted, Jenna refused to let the moment sweep her away.

Ignoring her racing pulse, she stepped back. It wasn't a huge step, but it was enough that the temperature around her cooled. "I think we'd better call it a night."

"Are you certain?" His expression was dangerously understanding.

"Yes, very."

"Very well. I will walk you to your door."

"The elevator will suffice." Truth be told, she didn't trust herself not to weaken if they made it anywhere near her bedroom. Already, she could feel the prickles of remorse nipping at her insides. That was the curse of leading with your head.

They resumed their walk in silence, the awareness from before replaced by a different kind of tension. "I'm sorry if you're disappointed," she caught herself saying, despite having nothing to apologize for.

He replied with a shrug. "*C'est la vie.* I told you before, I only go where I am invited."

"Dinner truly was lovely."

"I am glad you enjoyed yourself. Perhaps tomorrow I can impress you again. I thought you might like to tour the Pont du Gard and have a picnic by the river."

"Tomorrow?" Was he asking her out a second time? Even after she…?

"My ego is not so fragile that I would walk away from an interesting woman simply because she ended the evening early," he replied. "I have been in need of…company…this week, and you are exactly the breath of fresh air I was looking for. So, tomorrow. Shall I pick you up in the morning? The bridge is best enjoyed before the crowds."

"I—I had signed up for a bus tour." She meant the response as an excuse, but the words lacked conviction. Philippe made for a far better guide than any professionally run tour.

Plus, the prospect of seeing him again made her spine tingle. "Will nine o'clock work?" she asked him.

"Perfectly." His face brightened with satisfaction. "I shall see you then. And who knows? Perhaps tomorrow night you will reconsider issuing an invitation."

"Don't bet on it," she replied.

"Oh, but I like to gamble." Shivers passed through her at the way his voice dropped. "And now," he continued, "I will say good-night."

"But…we're not at the elevator."

"I know, but I thought it best we stop here."

"Why?" She looked around. They had stopped at the edge of the gardens, at a point where the pathway intersected with a concrete sidewalk. The door to the hotel was a few feet away, guarded by a pair of olive trees.

Fingers curled around the shell of her ear. "Because, *ma chère*, I plan to kiss you goodnight, and I prefer privacy."

Jenna's mouth ran dry. "Oh."

The kiss was gentle to start, as though he were waiting for her to kiss him back. Which Jenna quickly did, their lips sliding into a natural rhythm. The kisses grew deeper, and soon she found herself pressed tight against him, her hands clutching his shoulders.

No one had ever kissed her like this. With such passion and patience. He didn't grope or try to rush things to the next level. He just held her and tasted her as deeply as he could.

Until suddenly, abruptly, he broke away, leaving them both struggling to breathe again.

"Good night, Jenna," he whispered. "Sleep well."

After a kiss like that? Jenna wasn't sure that was possible.

Philippe couldn't remember the last time a woman rejected him and he went home smiling. Never? More proof that Jenna Brown was what he needed this week.

He inhaled, letting the jasmine and lavender fill him. Every season, the pungency caught him off guard. One would think, after a lifetime of harvests, he would remember. Hadn't he told Jenna one never forgets a perfume?

His brother loved the smell, as did his parents. Usually, the scent filled him with melancholy, but not tonight. Tonight, for the first time in a long time, the floral scent accompanied more pleasant thoughts.

Should he feel guilty, pursuing Jenna so ardently? After all, he was everything she oh-so-cynically accused him of being.

Then again, she was a grown woman, intelligent and strong enough to know whether she wanted to sleep with a man.

He ran a thumb across his lips. How enjoyable it would be if she invited him into her bed. He certainly looked forward to convincing her she should.

CHAPTER FOUR

"WHY DIDN'T YOU tell me you were afraid of heights?" Philippe asked.

"I'm not afraid of heights. It's narrow, circular stairs I don't like." One hundred forty very narrow stairs that were expected to accommodate both up and down traffic. Every few steps, Jenna found herself having to hug the railing in order to allow a descending tourist to pass.

"Relax." Philippe's voice sounded in her ear. "I'm standing right behind you. You're not going to get knocked over."

"You better hope not, because I'm pulling you down with me to break my fall," she told him.

They were in Nîmes, climbing the famed Tour Magne, a thousand-year-old tower that promised panoramic views of the city. It had been four days since their dinner on the terrace. Four days of romantic outings followed by Jenna sending Philippe home to sleep in his own bed despite wanting to do the opposite. No matter how enticing Philippe's kisses, a voice told her to hold back.

He was too perfect; that was the problem. Charming. Witty. Sexy. Always knowing what to say. And none of it dipping below the surface. Except for that one slip of a moment on the terrace, he kept his true self at bay, as much a stranger as the day they met—albeit a very enticing stranger.

At the top of the stairs, they passed through a doorway and onto a stone observation deck. "See?" Philippe said. "I told you the view was worth it."

He was right. All around them spread the city of Nîmes. Despite the dark clouds rolling in over the mountains, the view was spectacular. In the distance, Jenna could see the walls of the arena of Nîmes, the famous Roman amphitheatre, while if she looked down, she could see the walls and waterways of the public gardens. They made their way to a spot along the wall and stood one in front of the other, Philippe's arms holding her in place. "I see what you mean now about the gardens being designed so you can view them from above," she said.

"The tower wasn't originally this tall. After Rome conquered the area, Augustus doubled the height for protection purposes."

Of course, he knew such a fact. "Is there any piece of local history you don't know?"

"Not really."

"I feel spoiled, having my own walking, talking guidebook," she told him. One whose eyes lit up when sharing interesting facts. She wished they weren't standing back to front so she could see his eyes right now.

"We aim to please." His arms came around either side of her to rest on the top of the battlement.

Maybe standing back to front wasn't so bad after all.

She snuggled into his space while he pointed out landmarks and shared historical anecdotes.

"You should have been a history professor," she said after a while. She could imagine how popular he would be with university students. The waiting list for his class would be a mile long.

"Believe it or not, there was a time when I wanted to do just that."

"What made you change your mind?"

"The business needed me. My parents were gone. Felix's illness made it hard for him to keep on top of everything. Since I've a knack for numbers…"

"You stepped up to help."

"I had to. What good is D'Usay International without a d'Usay at the helm? Some of these companies have been dealing with our family for nearly a century."

"Tradition is important to you, isn't it? Forget I asked." The answer was obvious, given his passion for history.

A man who valued the past but lived for today. Quite the contradiction.

"When you belong to a family with deep roots, you cannot help but respect tradition. The d'Usay name has been an integral part of Provence's history."

With him being the last of them. "The pressure is on for you to boost the family numbers."

"Or let the name die out."

"You don't plan to have children?"

"Good Lord, no. Not on purpose, anyway."

"Really?" She was surprised. For someone who believed in honoring the past as much as he did, you'd think he'd want to preserve that history into the future for as long as he could.

"Children and relationships require commitment," he replied. "In case you haven't guessed, I prefer to stay as entanglement-free as possible."

Hopping from one good time to the next. Didn't that sound familiar? "You're not afraid you'll get bored? Even pleasure seeking has its limits."

"Not if you do it right," he teased.

Releasing her from his arms, he came around to face her. The wind had ruffled his curls, adding emphasis to his devil-may-care remarks. "Not everyone in the world is meant to settle down, *ma chère*."

"But what about your family legacy?" The history he so respected. How could he, on one hand, talk so reverently about his ancestors, and on the other, talk about never settling down?

"Families die out." As he spoke, a cloud passed in front of the sun, casting his face in shadows. "If the d'Usays were meant to continue, there'd be more family around than only me."

But if he had children… Jenna kept her thoughts to herself and instead stared out at the city below. Terra-cotta roofs and white marble dotted with evergreen spires. It wasn't Philippe's fault he'd picked at an emotional scab. What did it matter to her if he spent the her skin reached all the way to her toes. "I can make a stronger one, if you'd like."

Oh dear. Jenna's mouth ran dry.

Thunder rumbled in the distance. "It's going to storm," she managed to say.

The sky above them was quickly darkening. The tourists who'd been enjoying the view around them began filing their way down the stairs.

Philippe stopped her when she started to follow. "We have time," he told her.

"For what? Getting struck by lightning?"

"We will be fine. I want to take advantage of the privacy to finish explaining myself."

"I really don't think…"

He kissed her. *Oh.* That *explanation.*

Jenna fell into the kiss.

They got caught in the rain. A drenching downpour of a storm that left them soaked to the skin before they could sprint to the car. Hardly the romantic moment Philippe had planned for.

It was his fault, of course. He got caught up in the kiss and completely forgot about the advancing storm. Jenna's kisses had the strangest effect on him. The taste of her went straight

rest of his life jet-setting around the world? In fact, more power to him for being honest than misleading women with false hopes.

"You're frowning." Philippe's fingers played with the hair by her ear. "You're disappointed with me."

"Quite the opposite, actually. I was thinking of someone who should have taken a page from your book. Might have saved a whole lot of pain."

"Someone broke your heart?" His hand combed through her hair before coming to rest on her shoulder. "The man is a fool."

His sentiment made her smile. "Not my heart," she told him. "My mother's. My dad never should have married her. Unfortunately, he wasn't as forthright as you."

"I'm sorry."

"It is what it is. I figured out a long time ago I'm not responsible for my parents' mistakes." Not even if she was one of them. "You learn to deal."

Unless you were her mother, that was.

Jenna could feel Philippe's eyes on her as he waited for her to go on. She didn't want to. Talking about her family, even in the most vague of terms, depressed her, and she didn't want to spoil the afternoon.

"Anyway, you're right. Relationships take commitment, and if that's not your thing, more power to you for realizing before someone gets hurt."

"Precisely. Thank you for understanding."

Jenna shrugged. "I take it I'm one of the few?"

"There are women who consider my resolution a challenge," he said, "and therefore feel the need to take up the gauntlet, so to speak."

She could only imagine what the gauntlet entailed. "Let me guess. You don't let these women down gently."

"Sometimes bluntness is the only way to get the point across."

"What about you?" Philippe asked.

"What about me?"

"Are you looking for marriage and children?"

"Not with you, if that's what you're worried about," she replied. "But eventually, I suppose. If the right person comes along, and if his heart doesn't have vascular ADD."

"Vascular what?"

"It's a term Shirley and I came up with to describe guys who can't stay committed longer than a month before falling in love with someone else."

"Ah, I see. Well, I can promise you, I do not have vascular ADD. My heart doesn't wish to commit, period."

Leaning closer, he added in a low voice, "You realize you are making the perfect argument for our enjoying each other's company for the remainder of the week. Because we are both on the same page."

His logic was hard to follow with his breath tickling her neck. "Are we? On the same page?"

"I like to think so. Don't you?"

Jenna shouldn't have turned to meet his eyes. The promise in his voice already conjured up way too many delicious connotations. Falling into the purple, she felt her resolve fraying. It would be so easy to tumble and get lost, she thought. But, oh, how tempting.

"But if I say yes, then who's to say I'll see you again?" she asked. Surely part of his attraction was the challenge.

"You are far too interesting for me to lose interest in one night. I find myself wanting to know every bit of you. Inside…" He traced his index finger across her collarbone. "And out."

Jenna started to melt, the way she always did when he turned seductive. "You make a strong argument."

He caught her face. The feel of his palms on

to his head the way champagne used to when he was a boy. Only she tasted much sweeter.

He could only imagine what taking her to bed would be like.

From the passenger seat, Jenna flashed him a valiant smile. She was soaked. Water dripped from her curls and ran down the sides of her face, and her once brightly colored outfit stuck to her skin. Although he'd turned the air temperature as warm as he dared, goose bumps still covered her arms and legs. She looked miserable. Beautiful, but miserable.

He spied the road sign ahead and made an executive decision.

"I don't remember taking this turn on the drive in," she said.

"We didn't. I'm going to my apartment in Arles instead."

Right on cue, the wariness flashed across her face. "To dry off and get something to eat. Unless you'd rather stay in those wet clothes for an extra thirty minutes."

"Not really," she replied. There was a moment, though, when he saw her considering the option. Fortunately for them both, common sense won out.

"Then it's settled. We'll find you some dry clothes and I'll order us some dinner from

Chez Marguerite." The café on the corner was one of his favorite haunts. His living room looked out on the amphitheater. He could set up a small table so they could enjoy the view.

Amazing, how much he enjoyed entertaining her. Yes, part of his enthusiasm was driven by a desire to seduce. He'd never met a woman so determined to keep him at arm's length. Well, not quite arm's length, or they wouldn't be soaked to the skin. But, the last day or so, his desire had taken on another layer. He *liked* her. She challenged him intellectually, something his usual dates never did, and when he spoke about history, she listened. Actively listened, not the lip service he so often received. Surprised him to admit it, but if their time together never progressed beyond a few kisses and good company, he would still consider the week a success.

Of course, their time together could be far richer if they explored each other as well as the region. If only she would let herself go.

It was still raining buckets when they pulled up in front of his building. "So much for drying in the car," Jenna said as they raced up the front steps. "I think my sneakers are going to squish for days."

"We will throw everything in the dryer.

It'll be dry in no time." He tossed his keys on the table by the front door, next to a stack of mail. The house was hot and muggy after being locked up for several days, making his wet clothes feel ten times heavier.

Jenna, meanwhile, stood by the door, hugging her frame. Her arms glistened with rainwater. So did her face. Her lips. It was all he could do not to kiss the moisture from her skin.

"Come with me," he said, reaching for her hand.

"Where are we going?"

"To get you out of those wet clothes." She was far too tempting in them.

He led her upstairs to his en suite. Thankfully, the housekeeper had cleaned up before taking the week off. Grabbing his robe from behind the bathroom door, he handed it to her.

"This should keep you warm while your clothes are drying. There are fresh towels in the bathroom as well, if you'd like to take a shower to warm up. Or I could draw you a bath…"

He liked how her brows knit together as he pointed out the tub. "It looks big enough to swim in," she said.

"It's meant for two people. But in this case, I'm merely offering an opportunity to get warm," he quickly added. "I will be downstairs ordering dinner."

"Thanks, but the towel and the robe are fine. I don't think I need to go swimming in your tub right now."

"The choice is up to you. You can always change your mind later." Because he couldn't help himself, he combed the wet hair from her face. "You can have anything you want this evening. All you have to do is ask."

Philippe was whistling in a room on the second floor when Jenna stepped out of the bedroom. Clutching her wet clothes, she padded her way toward the sound. His "apartment," as he called it, was really a narrow antique house with the main living quarters on the upper floors. Philippe's bedroom occupied the bulk of the third floor.

It was gorgeous. Elegant and masculine, much like the man himself. The entire time she was undressing, Jenna had been painfully aware that she stood feet away from the bed he slept in. When she wrapped his robe around her body, his scent had enveloped her, too. All of it reminding her that all she need to do was ask.

She found him at the far end of the second floor in what had to be the living room. Again, the decor reeked of wealthy masculinity. Leather furniture. High-end electronics. The perfect bachelor apartment.

While she'd been upstairs, he'd managed to find dry clothes of his own—a pair of striped linen pants and a shirt that hung loose. He was moving a small table from the corner to in front of the terrace window, the exertion causing his shirtsleeves to tighten around bulging biceps.

Jenna coughed the sudden frog from her throat. "What would you like me to do with these?"

"I'll take them downstairs." He looked her up and down with a grin. "You wear that robe well."

"I feel like a character from those science fiction movies." The long garment pooled around her feet, and the sleeves wouldn't stay rolled.

"You'll have your own clothes soon enough. I poured us some wine. It's by the fireplace."

Sure enough, two glasses of red wine sat on the fireplace mantel. "You've been busy," she called after him. How long had she lingered in his bedroom?

There was a photograph on the mantel as

well. One of those formal family shots like the ones on display at the hotel, only this one was more recent. In it, a middle-aged man stood behind a sofa, his hand on the shoulder of a beautiful dark-haired woman. A young boy of about eight sat next to her, while she held a baby on her lap.

Philippe's family.

She spied another frame by a lamp. Of two men in bathing suits this time. They stood on the beach, the older one with his arm hooked around the younger boy's shoulders. Despite the fact both men wore sunglasses, Jenna recognized Philippe's grin immediately. He'd clearly been a charmer since birth.

"That was in St. Tropez." Philippe returned from the kitchen with plates in his hands. "My parents insisted on a family holiday before Felix returned to the university."

"You look like you're having a good time."

"That was the last time we were all together. My father flew to Milan in the morning. He was struck by a car leaving his hotel a few days later."

No wonder he displayed the photo. Carefully, she set the frame back on the mantel. Meanwhile, Philippe was busying himself by setting the table, carefully arranging the two plates as though hosting a formal dinner. "I thought you might prefer a view while eating. Ideally, I would have preferred to enjoy the fading sun, but it is still better than the dining room."

"You don't like talking about family, do you?"

"*Pardon?*"

She'd been around enough difficult conversations, not to mention ducking more than a few herself, to recognize avoidance tactics when she saw them. Philippe's sad family history was none of her business, but the sadness in his voice when he mentioned his father's death called to her. Just like when he mentioned his brother the other evening, she saw a glimmer of what lurked beneath his perfect surface, and the sight had her wanting more. To quote someone in the room, she wanted to know him inside and out.

"Whenever the topic comes up, you change the subject. It's happened three times now."

"Has it?" He shifted one of the plates an inch to the left. "Interesting you should notice, seeing as how you do the same thing."

Touché. "That's different," Jenna replied.

"How so?"

"Your family is worth talking about."

Her comment, which came out before she could censor herself, hung in the silence, waiting for elaboration. There was no way Philippe would let her move on until she did. Not after she'd challenged his reluctance to share. Taking a long drink of wine for fortification, she thought of how to best explain.

"My mom stopped living the day my dad moved out," she started.

"I'm confused. I thought your mother was alive."

"She is, but there's a difference between being alive and living."

"I see."

"She wakes up, she works, she does all the things she's supposed to do, but…" Jenna's hand tightened on the goblet. As was the case whenever she talked about her mother, she felt the frustration squeezing at her throat. "It's like she hit pause the day he moved out and has been on hold ever since. Waiting for my father to come home." Never moving forward. Never giving up hope. "Twenty freaking years."

"And your father? Does he know?"

"Oh, he knows all right, and he *loves* it. Encourages it, actually. Every few years, he pops up, like a bad penny. Usually around the time his current relationship is on the rocks, and he needs an ego stroking. Last I heard, he was shacking up with some girl half his age. To be honest, I lose track."

"He has a lot of relationships."

"He is a jerk," Jenna replied. "He uses women, makes promises he has no intention of keeping and is out the door as soon as something better comes along." Thinking of him left a bad taste in her mouth. "Pretty sure the only reason he stuck it out with my mother for as long as he did was because Grandpa threatened to kill him."

"Must have been very hard for you growing up."

Jenna swallowed the mouthful of rosé she'd gulped. "I caught on to his bogus promises in the sixth grade. Mom, though…" She shook her head. A lifetime wasted waiting on a man who didn't love anyone but himself. "See why I'm not keen on talking about my family? At least your family accomplished things. Your father loved your mother. My mother sat on the sofa waiting." She stared into her glass.

"Maybe she waited because she didn't know what else to do?"

"Clearly." She let out a harsh breath. "I'd understand if my father were some kind of prize, but he isn't."

The sofa sagged as Philippe joined her. A moment later, his arm wrapped around her shoulders, pulling her close.

Leaning on him was dangerously natural.

"My mother sketched," he said.

"I beg your pardon?" His comment didn't make much sense given their conversation.

"After my father's accident, my mother took up drawing. Day in, day out, she sketched things. Fruit. Furniture. Page after page of unrecognizable objects. You might say it was a compulsion."

"Why?"

"Felix asked the same question. She told him it was to make the day go by faster. She didn't know what else to do with herself. Felix took over my father's job. Her job had been to take care of my father."

"And you," Jenna replied. "Weren't you only a teenager?"

"Yes, but I also had the life of a teenager. I didn't need my mother the way I once did."

His fingers combed through her hair as he talked. "Perhaps your mother waits because she doesn't know how to draw."

Jenna didn't know what to say. When she first mentioned the photograph, she hadn't expected the conversation to turn into a bearing of souls. But, here they were, sharing.

Lifting her head, she looked at Philippe and was taken aback by the seriousness of his expression. How beautiful he looked when stripped of all pretenses. It was a face she imagined the world seldom got to see, and she was honored he showed himself to her.

A wall shifted inside her. She'd been attracted to Philippe since first glance, but the attraction was deeper now. Underpinned by a layer of connection that came from two people sharing their hidden selves.

Suddenly, she wanted to be closer. In a few days, she would be back in Nantucket, and she wanted this night, this closeness, to be the memory she carried home.

"Philippe?" she whispered. "Do you remember when you said I could have anything I wanted?"

She caught him by the chin, forcing him to meet her gaze. Watching the violet slowly turn to indigo as he realized what she was saying. "I'm asking."

Jenna woke to an empty bed and the sound of Philippe on the phone speaking in rapid French. When he saw her sitting up, he winked and pointed to a tray on the dresser where a carafe of coffee and two mugs sat. After shaking the sleep from her curls, Jenna padded over to pour a cup.

"*Dits Pierre d'embaucher quelques mains supplémentaires s'il est en désavantage numérique. Nous ne pouvons pas tomber en retard sur l'horaire. Dior s'attend à tout pour être envoyées par la huitième,*" she heard Philippe say.

He could be discussing plumbing fixtures for all she knew, but it didn't matter. The language sounded beautiful dripping off his tongue. Setting herself on the end of the bed, she watched how the muscles played across his bare back each time he gestured with his arms. Memories of different, soft French words came back to her. Words of encouragement and pleasure. The muscles in his arms flexed, reminding her how they'd held her close.

"*Je suis désolé, ma chérie,*" Philippe said when his conversation was finished. "I am sorry. They are behind schedule in delivering the lavender to the distillery. The oil isn't perfect unless the flowers are at their freshest. We already have enough competition with Egypt undercutting us on price. The least we can do is deliver on time." He set the phone aside and joined her on the bed. "I told them I would go back and cut the branches myself."

"Would you?" she asked.

"It would not be the first time. And good morning." Leaning in, he gave her a lingering kiss before slipping the coffee from her hands and helping himself to a sip. "Did you sleep well?"

"Very."

"Good. I am glad. I apologize for not letting you sleep in, but as it turns out, it's for the best that you're awake. I wasn't joking about heading back to supervise the harvest."

So much for her keeping him interested. Having finally succeeded in seducing her, he was saying goodbye. No more reason to play tour guide. "You want to head back to the valley."

"I'm afraid I don't have a choice. My absence is part of the reason they have slowed down, so I need to make an appearance. Which is why it is good that you're awake. Now we have time to see a bit of Arles after breakfast."

"You're still playing tour guide?"

He cocked his head. Their night had left his hair wavy and askew, making him more beautiful than ever. "Unless you'd rather take a swim in my tub," he teased.

Was he serious? There wasn't going to be a quick goodbye? No morning drop-off at the hotel with a kiss before he drove out of her life?

"You're frowning again," he said, brushing a thumb across her lips. "You didn't believe me yesterday, did you?"

"I…"

"I told you yesterday. You are far too interesting to let go after one night. You don't leave for five more days, correct? The way I see things, that means we have five more days to enjoy each other's company. That is, if you enjoyed last night." His knuckle caught her chin. "Did you? Enjoy it?"

Jenna nodded. She was getting lost in his stare again. Those magnetic violet eyes were going to be the death of her.

He smiled. "So did I, *ma chérie*. So did I."

CHAPTER FIVE

As far as Philippe was concerned, it wasn't unusual for him to have a lover stay around the morning after. He'd even been known to enjoy a romantic weekend or two. But he'd never found himself eager to spend an entire week with someone, let alone two. While he'd begun this venture looking for a few days' distraction, he hadn't anticipated being so thoroughly entertained.

They ended up in the tub after all, the notion of seeing Jenna glistening wet again too enticing to pass up. Later, they lingered over coffee and croissants as they waited for the market to open. There he helped her pick out French perfume. He'd been right that first evening. Jasmine did suit her.

The entire time, he could tell, she was waiting for him to say goodbye. Therefore, it was no surprise to see her eyes widen when he drove past the hotel entrance and headed straight to Château d'Usay.

"You would rather go to your room?" he asked.

"Eventually," she replied. "Seeing as how that's where my clothes are."

He thought of telling her not to worry about something she wouldn't need, but thought better. "We'll go together once I finish my meeting. Do you mind waiting?"

"No. If you don't mind me giving myself a private tour. I missed a few rooms when I was here earlier in the week."

That was when it hit him how much time they'd spent together. Five days had never passed so quickly. Suddenly five more didn't seem like enough.

The meeting lasted longer than he intended. In an effort to keep costs low, Pierre, his manager, had hired fewer workers, a mistake, as it turned out. Now they were going to be forced to pay for extra help at the height of harvest season and recalculate their production schedule.

As a result, two hours passed before he returned to the house.

"Jenna, are you here?" The quiet upon entering made him nervous. She might have gotten bored and gone back to the hotel on her own.

"In the room next to the salon," she called out.

His great-grandfather's library. He found her curled up in the desk chair studying the photos that lined the bookshelves behind her. For a moment, he simply stood in the doorway. The desk was near the back window where it got the afternoon sun. Flecks of dust floated in the beam like tiny little lights. It was like looking at an angel.

"My mother used to call this room a dust-collecting nuisance," he said, finally announcing his presence.

She looked up, and the smile she greeted him with took his breath away. *"Tu es belle,"* he caught himself saying.

"I really need to brush up on my French," she replied. The blush on her cheeks said she guessed at the meaning, if not the literal translation.

Interesting that she would blush at his compliments now.

Strolling to the desk, he saw that one of the photographs rested on her lap. It was his parents by the Eiffel Tower. "I believe that was taken on their honeymoon."

"They look very happy."

"*Oui.* They loved each other very much. They were always laughing and enjoying themselves." Until his father died and his mother stopped laughing, that is. He took the photo out of her hands. "In many ways, she is like your mother. Part of her died with him. Perhaps that is why she didn't put up a fight when she got sick."

"How did she die?" Jenna's question was soft and hesitant.

"Meningitis. It was very quick. One day she had a terrible headache and a stiff neck. A few days later, she was gone."

A thickness filled the air, not unlike the thickness in his throat. Jenna reached across the space and touched his arm. No words. Just a touch. Philippe felt more comfort than he had in years.

"When I think of how quickly she died, I tell myself it is a good reminder that we should pack as much living into our days as possible."

"You do a good job," she replied.

"Since I'm the only one left, I have to live for three. Did you finish your tour?"

"Pretty much." She put the photo back in its spot. "You definitely have a lot of family history to unpack. Between the castle and here,

I'm realizing your family didn't just live for centuries—they were involved in every major historical event in France. I envy you. My family's more of a mishmash of mistakes. The part I know of, anyway."

Philippe wanted to say that not everyone knew their family's roots as intricately as he did, but he held back. Jenna tended to share very little of herself. He wanted to see if she'd share more.

She did. "I never met my dad's family," she told him. "I asked once, during one of my parents' reunions, but all he said was that he didn't talk to them. The grandparents I do know? Total pieces of work. Grandma did nothing but complain when they visited. About Grandpa. About how pathetic my mom is."

"Didn't your grandfather say something?"

"He was too busy complaining about my grandmother." She smiled. "Made for some fun Christmas dinners. Especially when my uncles and their wives came around."

"I can imagine." Actually, he couldn't. What she described sounded like a horribly toxic environment. How on earth had it produced such a preppy little angel? No wonder her friend Beatrice gave her an adventure. If ever a woman was in need of fun memories, it was Jenna.

Made him more determined than ever to make sure the remainder of her trip was as memorable as possible.

"There is one thing your family did right," he said.

She came around to his side of the desk to sit on the edge. "Really? What's that?"

"They created you."

Pink crept into her cheeks. She doubted him, but he meant the compliment. For all the issues her parents had, or in spite of them, they'd raised someone special. "Flattery will get you everywhere, Monsieur d'Usay," she told him.

"Is that so? I'm glad to hear it." He dipped his head for a kiss. "What do you say we continue this tour upstairs? There are a few rooms you haven't seen."

"And what rooms would those be?" As she asked the question, she hooked her fingers through his belt loop and pulled him toward her. For a woman who only a day earlier had been dodging his advances, the brazenness was an amazing turn. Snagging her belt loops in return, he tugged her to her feet. "To begin? My bedroom."

Sunrise had never looked so beautiful. Jenna watched as inch by inch, the fields outside her hotel room turned from blue to gold and purple. If she could only stop time from moving forward. Not forever. Only for a few more days.

She was going to miss Provence. The smells, the sounds, the people. She felt at home here in a way she couldn't explain. The feeling went beyond the man in her bed. The region itself spoke to her.

Philippe's arms slipped around her waist, wrapping her in warmth. "What are you doing awake so early?" He pressed his lips to her temple. "Come back to bed."

"I have to leave for the airport in a few hours," she replied.

"Six hours. We have plenty of time yet."

Six hours didn't sound like plenty of time to her. She couldn't believe her trip was almost over. The final few days had passed in a blur of sunny days and too-short nights. Tomorrow she would be back in Nantucket, going to bed. Alone.

"I wish this week didn't have to end," she said.

"Mmm…" Philippe was too busy peppering her jaw and neck with kisses. "Then cancel your flight. Stay a few more days."

If only she could. "I can't. I have to be back at work day after tomorrow."

"I'll get you a new job."

"While I appreciate the…er…offer…" Philippe's lips had moved to the curve of her shoulder. "I think I need to stick to the original plan." Even if it were possible, a few more days would only be postponing the inevitable. Besides, she was already perilously close to letting the affair cross into emotional territory. Sharing secrets in the dark, it was easy to forget this was a vacation fling. Every time Philippe shared some moment from his life, Jenna could feel herself slipping deeper under his spell.

Far better she leave as scheduled. Before she made a fool out of herself and actually fell in love with the man.

"If that is the case, then I insist you come back to bed," Philippe said. "So I can leave you with a proper memory for the flight home."

Who was Jenna to argue with creating another memory?

"Have I thanked you for such an amazing week?" she asked as he led her away from the window.

They reached the bed, and he sat down on the edge, trapping her between his knees. Jenna gasped as his fingers brushed the backs of her legs. "Last night while we were dancing on the terrace, but you can thank me again, if you'd like."

"I'm never going to forget this trip for as long as I live," she said. *God bless Beatrice.*

"Should I take that to mean you had a proper adventure?"

"Let's see... Roman ruins, champagne under the stars, a sexy French lover. Most definitely. I have been well and truly spoiled."

A expression she couldn't recognize softened his features. "You deserve to be spoiled, *ma chérie*. I am glad you chose Provence for your adventure."

"Me too." Smiling back the lump in her throat, she combed her fingers through his dark waves. "It was the trip of a lifetime. I'll never forget it."

"And I shall remember you, Jenna Brown. Very fondly."

For a little while, maybe. Jenna wouldn't fool herself into thinking she would dwell in his memory forever. A few weeks from now, another woman would be in his bed, while she went on with her life. It was how holiday affairs worked.

Until she stepped through those airport

doors, though, Philippe was still hers. And he'd promised her another memory.

She climbed onto his lap.

Philippe watched the crowded checkpoint until he could no longer see Jenna's copper-colored head. That was that. The week was over. A heaviness settled in his stomach. He would miss his little American. Too bad she'd never know how much he appreciated her passing through his life or how she'd managed to return pleasure to harvest week. There were times, usually when they were lying together in the dark, when he was struck by how well they blended together. Like the notes of a perfume. Strong enough that he almost—almost—suggested he fly to Nantucket to see her again. Thankfully he came to his senses. What had drawn him to Jenna was her difference from the other women in his world. But that difference was also why he shouldn't see her again. Beneath her cynical exterior was a woman who believed in love and forever. The kind of woman men fell in love with.

The kind of woman he avoided.

In the end, it was best he leave Jenna Brown

and her enticing smile here at the airport and go back to his routine.

He wished her a wonderful life. She deserved it.

September

Jenna sat on the linoleum floor watching the second hand sweep across the clock. One minute. Two minutes.

Her breathing matched the steady pace. In one second, out the next. In, out. In, out. She wanted to close her eyes but was too afraid she'd lose count of the time.

Twenty seconds. Thirty seconds.

Ninety-nine percent accurate, the package said. She didn't really need a package. She already knew the answer. Two weeks of procrastinating had her pretty certain. Still, nothing was one hundred percent—not even the test, apparently.

Forty-five seconds.

Her heart was racing. The slow breathing wasn't helping. In fact, trying to breathe slowly caused a tightening in her chest. A knot the size of her fist blocked the air from flowing comfortably.

Fifty-five seconds.

She looked down at the stick in her hand. A bright blue plus sign peered up at her through the result window.

Pregnant.

"Do you have any plans to actually eat that?"

"Huh?" Jenna looked up from her plate to find her friend watching her intently. They were sitting at their favorite restaurant having lunch. Peak tourist season was over, meaning they could enjoy an ocean-view table. On the other side of the glass, the harbor was quiet. At this point in the year, island traffic slowed except for the weekends.

Shirley pointed to Jenna's plate. "Your salmon," she said. "You've been stabbing it for the past five minutes. Is there a reason why you're mutilating it?"

"Teaching it a lesson?" Jenna offered before setting down her fork. "Sorry. I got lost in thought."

"No kidding. You barely reacted when I mentioned Joe asked me to go to New York City with him for the weekend." Joseph Kwan being the lawyer Shirley had recently started dating.

"He did?"

"See? I knew you weren't listening. And yes, he did. We're going Columbus Day weekend."

"That's fantastic," Jenna replied. Good for Shirley for making a meaningful connection. "Just be careful. Don't do anything stupid."

Retrieving her fork, she started poking at her fish again. "Are you sure you're okay?" Shirley asked. "You've been acting weird since you returned from France. You're not hung up on that guy you met, are you?"

"Philippe. His name was Philippe, and the two of us were clear from the start that once the holiday ended, so did we."

Seven weeks had passed since Jenna came back from France, long enough for the memories of her trip to recede. Some memories, anyway.

Some would stick with her forever.

What was Philippe doing now? It was evening in France. Was he with a woman?

Who was she kidding? Of course he was with a woman. Someone beautiful and sophisticated.

Looking down, she saw her knuckles had turned white from squeezing the fork.

"I don't mean to be distracted," she told Shirley, setting the fork down again. "I've got a bunch of stuff on my mind, is all." Three little sticks, all with the same double blue lines.

"Anything I can do to help? It's not family stuff, is it?"

"Kind of. The thing is…" She stopped herself. Philippe deserved to be the first to know. She'd been avoiding calling him for a week, telling herself it was because she didn't know the right words. What would he say? Would he be happy?

"The thing is what?" Shirley asked.

"Something I need to handle on my own," Jenna replied. And soon. The time for procrastinating was over. There were decisions to be made.

Her stomach started churning. On her plate, the once attractive piece of fish had become a pile of pink chunks smothered in apricot sauce. Jenna grabbed her water to keep the sour taste from rising in her throat.

"I'm sorry," she apologized to her friend. "I'm not feeling well. Do you mind if I bail?"

"Sure. Let's flag down the waitress."

"No. You stay and finish your meal. No sense in both of us ruining our lunch." Besides, she needed to be alone to formulate her thoughts.

"If you're sure," Shirley said. When it came

to food, she was easily convinced. "Call me later and let me know how you're feeling?"

"Sure."

It would be the second call Jenna made.

The first would be to France, to let Philippe know that the d'Usay family line wasn't going to die out after all.

She had her phone out before she stepped through her front door, only to catch herself before hitting the dial button. What would he say when she told him? Would he believe her or, would he think it a trick? He was a well-known millionaire; it wasn't inconceivable to think a woman might try and score a payday.

Jenna took a deep breath. In the end, it didn't matter if he thought she was trying to trick him, did it? She was pregnant, and he was the father.

She dialed.

"*Allo*?" The sound of his voice swept over her, taking her breath away. She'd forgotten how smooth and melodic it was.

"*Allo*?" he repeated.

"Hel…" She found her voice. "Hello, Philippe? This is Jenna. Jenna Brown. From Nantucket."

"Jenna?" Was it her imagination or did he sound happy to hear her voice? It was hard to tell because of the background noise. He was in a restaurant or at a party or somewhere. She could hear the voices and the sound of cutlery.

Oh God, he was on a date. "Is…is this a bad time?"

"No, no. Is something wrong?"

"Well," she said, wincing, "that depends on your definition of wrong. I'm pregnant."

Silent greeted her announcement. She might have thought they were disconnected except for the crowd noise. "Philippe? Did you hear…?"

"Are you certain?"

Jenna's heart sank. Stupid her. Apparently a small part of her had held out hope that he'd be excited about the news. "I took the test three times. I'm going to take a blood test this week to make sure." The test was more of a formality than confirmation at this point.

"That is a good idea," Philippe said. "To be certain, I mean. You'll call me when you get the results?"

"Of course. As soon as I know them."

"*Merci.* I would appreciate that."

He might as well have been asking her to call about a flower order, for all the emotion in his voice. *He doesn't want his dinner companion to know his business.* Again her stomach sank, and again she kicked herself for being disappointed. "I know this is probably the last thing you were expecting," she said. "I'm still trying to wrap my head around the news myself. It was as big a surprise to me, I assure you."

"I—I'm sure."

"Anyway, I thought you should know."

"*Oui. Merci.* That is, thank you for telling me. You will call when you have the results?"

Jenna nodded. "As soon as I have them," she said into the phone.

"Good. *Merci.* I'll talk to you soon, then."

Hopefully that call would go better. This call was so awkward it hurt. It more ways than one. "I should probably let you get back to your meal," she said.

"How did you…?"

"I can hear the silverware."

"Ah."

Silence filled the line again. Jenna wished she could see his face to know what he was thinking. The flatness of his voice left no clue.

"Good night, then," she said.

"Jenna…"

Her thumb froze. "Yes?"

"Nothing. Good night."

The dial tone kept her from saying any more.

Well, it was done, she thought, as she let the phone slip from her ear. He knew.

Philippe hung up the phone and returned to his seat in the restaurant. The crowd, which had been loud and boisterous before Jenna's call, had faded as though someone pushed the entire setting into the background.

A baby. His baby.

"Is something wrong? You look like you saw a ghost."

Shaking himself from his fog, he smiled at his dinner companion. "No ghost, Xavier, just unexpected news."

"Good news, I hope," his friend replied.

"I—" He wasn't sure. "I think so."

He was still trying to absorb the phone call. For the last few years, Philippe had told himself he would be the end of the d'Usay line. That there would be no wife, no child, *no heir* to carry on the family tradition.

Now, thanks to Jenna, that was no longer the case. There was going to be another d'Usay after all. The concept filled him with an emotion he couldn't describe. All of a sudden he felt…happy.

At the opposite end of the table, his lawyer Xavier Cousteau was carving up his steak.

"How strong are you when it comes to family law?" he asked him.

"Not very. I studied it in law school, but my knowledge doesn't go much further," Xavier replied. "Why?"

"I'm going to need a person who can help me establish a trust." A trust. A support plan. His mind was ticking off steps. "Can you find me someone?"

"*Oui.* Of course. But why?"

"Because, my friend…" Philippe paused while he signaled the server. When the man approached, he asked for two glasses of malt whisky.

"Philippe?" Xavier prodded.

"Because," Philippe replied, "it's time for me to start thinking about the future."

CHAPTER SIX

October

MORNING SICKNESS WAS the worst. For the past week, her stomach revolted every morning at five thirty. The only thing that quelled the nausea was a sweet cheese croissant from the bakery next to her apartment. Leaning over the sink in the break room, Jenna inhaled the pastry in two bites like she was trying to hide a dirty little secret.

"You're definitely part French," she told her stomach. Eight weeks in, her abdomen was still flat. For now. If she kept scarfing down pastry, she was going to gain twenty-five pounds in the first trimester alone.

Shirley poked her head through the door just as Jenna was washing her hands. "Mr. Mylanski was complaining of discomfort. I went ahead and gave him his morphine."

Poor old man's pain was getting worse.

"Thanks." She'd check in on him before she left to make sure he was sleeping.

"No problem. I saw you duck in here and figured you needed a second. Morning sickness strike again?"

"Uh-huh. Guess this means the pregnancy is a reality," she joked. "I was armed today, though. I bought an extra croissant. I should be fine until end of shift."

"Have you heard any more from…?"

The pastry grew heavy in her stomach. "Not since our last conversation."

She and Philippe had spoken twice. Once when she took the home pregnancy tests and again when the blood test made the pregnancy official. Both times he treated her like a business call, his tone flat and emotionless. One hundred and eighty degrees from the man she knew in France.

Could she blame him? Hadn't she stood on the Tour Magne and listened to him say he didn't want children?

In case you haven't guessed, I prefer to stay as entanglement-free as possible, he'd said.

He was in shock. When she called to report the blood test, he'd replied by saying, "I don't understand. We used protection."

"Nothing is one hundred percent," she'd reminded him. "And neither were we. Remember?"

The morning she departed France, when they'd been eager to make one last memory.

They made one, all right.

His silence had told her he remembered, and was kicking himself for getting carried away.

"What do you want to do?" had been the second thing he asked.

"I—I don't know," had been her reply. At the time she'd been as shocked as he was.

But, as her mind—and body—got used to the idea, she came to a conclusion. She wanted the baby, whether Philippe wanted to play a role in its life or not.

"You'll come first, too, I promise you that." She patted her stomach. "If your father doesn't want to be around, that's his loss. We'll live our lives just fine without him." The little life growing inside her belly would be the start of her new family legacy.

The floor was quiet when she stepped out of the break room. Always was this time of morning. Most of the patients were still asleep. Jenna stifled a yawn. Thirty minutes and she could get some sleep. Between working nights and the new pregnancy hormones, she was wiped. Lord help her when she reached the last trimester. Especially since she'd be carrying an extra two hundred pounds of pastry weight.

She was sitting at the nursing station, focused on logging patient notes, when the elevator door dinged. The morning shift had started to arrive. "Give me five minutes and I'll be ready to catch you up," she said, eyes focused on the computer screen.

A shadow crossed her desk. "Hello, Jenna."

It was Philippe.

Eight weeks hadn't changed much. Other than a few wrinkles in his dark suit, he looked as breathtakingly handsome as he had when they met.

Jenna's pulse stuttered. "What are you doing here?" In Nantucket. At the crack of dawn.

"It's good to see you, too." He smiled, but it lacked the sparkle she remembered. "Your custodian let me in. I think he thought I was here to see a patient."

"That's because family members are allowed twenty-four hours a day." Jenna didn't care how he'd gained entrance. She was way more interested in how he'd found her. "How did you know where I would be?"

"There's only one nursing home on your island. It wasn't too difficult," he replied. "And you mentioned how you often work overnights. How are you feeling?"

Really? He thought they would simply chat like nothing was wrong? "You don't speak to me for almost a week and then show up at my place of work unannounced. How do you think I feel?"

"I meant…" His eyes dropped to her midsection. "You look tired."

"Happens when you've worked all night." She left out the morning sickness.

"Of course," he replied. "I should have realized."

Meanwhile, he looked amazing.

God, but this was awkward. What happened to the easiness they shared in Provence? *Oh, right.* Her hand pressed to her stomach.

Philippe cleared his throat. "I'm sorry for…"

He was interrupted by a loud moan coming from one of the rooms. Mrs. Symonds. The elderly woman always moaned for several minutes upon waking.

"Morning, Mrs. Symonds," she heard Shirley say in a cheerful voice. "I'm going to visit you in about five minutes to give you your morning pill."

Her friend's shoes squeaked on the linoleum

as she rounded the corner and stopped short. "Well, isn't this a surprise," she said.

Philippe tilted his head. *"Pardon?"*

"This is my friend Shirley," Jenna said. "Shirley, this is Philippe d'Usay."

He reached for her hand, shaking it politely, not kissing it as he had done Jenna's the day they met. "You are the woman with the shingles. I trust you have healed?"

Shirley looked as surprised as Jenna felt. The last thing she expected was for Philippe to remember those kinds of details.

"Right as rain," she replied before shifting gears and moving into protective mode. Eyes narrowed, arms crossed in front of her chest, she assessed Philippe up and down like he was a stray dog. "Funny, but Jenna didn't mention you were coming to the island."

"I didn't know he was coming," Jenna responded. "It was a surprise."

"Really? How interesting."

"Tell me about it." To Philippe, she added, "I'll be wrapping up my shift in a few minutes. We can talk after that."

"Very good." He nodded. "I will wait for you outside."

As soon as he disappeared behind the elevator doors, Jenna's composure vanished.

"Are you going to be all right?" Shirley poured her a glass of water.

"I… I don't know." She honestly hadn't thought she'd ever see him again. Now that she had, her insides were a jumbled mess. "I suppose he wants to finish our discussion in person."

"Mighty nice of him, seeing as how he has fifty percent of the responsibility. This is a good sign, though, his showing up. Means he's stepping up."

"Maybe." Jenna was too mixed up to theorize. Whatever the reason, she'd have to wait until after her shift to find out.

Who knows? Maybe her nerves would have dissipated by then.

Along with the strange ache in her chest that arrived the same moment Philippe did.

Philippe took a seat on a bench just outside the nursing room door. The autumn air was brisk and damp; the sun hadn't been up long enough to burn away the fog. Employees walked past, barely giving him a moment's notice. How many of them knew Jenna? All of them? He imagined her being a popular coworker.

His head ached. He'd never been good at sleeping on planes, and this last flight was no exception. Too anxious about seeing Jenna, he'd tossed and turned the entire trip. A decent cup of coffee would help. Whatever the black liquid was that he purchased at the local airport did not count.

They'd had the most marvelous coffee that morning after in Arles. He smiled remembering how they'd strolled to the corner café for café au lait. Jenna's hair had been damp from the bath, her face freshly scrubbed and shining. Neither of them could stop grinning. You'd have thought they were a pair of virgin newlyweds the morning after their wedding night.

What did Jenna think of their week together now? Was it still a fond memory, or did she regret meeting him? His chest grew tight at the thought.

As if his thoughts conjured her, the door slid open and Jenna stepped outside. He was struck, just as he had been upstairs, by the fact his memory hadn't embellished the uniqueness of her beauty.

In France, she'd favored bright colors and comfortable, modest clothing. The American version was no different. Her uniform was a bright purple over which she wore a heavy knit cardigan. Together they hid her shape. No matter, his brain filled in the gaps.

Instinctively, he stood to kiss her hello, catching himself. If he'd only had this kind of restraint their last morning together...

He settled for an apology. "I'm sorry for showing up unannounced. I should have called and let you know I was coming."

"Yes, you should have. In fact, you should have called, period." Arms crossed over her chest, she glared at him with fiery green eyes. This was not, Philippe reminded himself, the time to be aroused by her feistiness. Before he could do or say anything, he needed to rectify the mistake he made by not communicating with her this past week.

"You are right. I've been in the UK on business and wanted to wait to talk in person. Still, that is no excuse."

"No, it isn't."

He could see he had some ground to make up. "Well, I am here now, and I want to deal with this."

"*This* is a baby."

"*Oui*, I know it is a baby." *His* baby. No matter how many times he repeated the phrase, the words continued to sound surreal. "Forgive me, I'm still in shock. I never expected to have a child."

She continued to glare, but her features softened slightly. "I suppose I've had a little more time to get used to the idea."

"A little," he replied.

The awkwardness between them was killing him. On the flight over, he'd mentally rewritten what he wanted to say until he had the perfect speech. Those words had vanished. All he could think about was how lovely she looked in the early-morning light. "Is there somewhere we can go to talk? I could use a drink."

"At seven thirty in the morning? Good luck." For the first time in their reunion, Jenna cracked a smile. "You'll have to settle for coffee."

"Coffee will do." Anything that let him clear his head.

They walked, in awkward silence, to a coffee shop a few blocks away. Looking around, Philippe took in Jenna's world. Nantucket was not Provence. The air tasted salty. The landscape was more rugged. There was a sense of pragmatism to the surroundings, he'd noticed, even with the most elegant of homes.

Despite it being a workday, the coffee shop was fairly empty. Only a handful of people waited in line to order. "Things quiet down here once summer is over," Jenna told him. "Plus, the only people around at this hour are locals heading to work. We can sit out on the deck and we won't be disturbed."

He let her lead the way to discover the small wooden structure overlooked a marsh pond filled with squawking birds. On a sunny day, the view was probably quite beautiful.

"You never answered my question about how you were feeling," he said once they'd settled in at one of the white plastic tables. She had refused his offer of coffee in favor of a sweet cheese pastry and a cup of warm water with honey and lemon. "You aren't suffering any kind of complications or anything?"

"Nothing sweet cheese croissants won't cure. Morning sickness," she clarified when he frowned. "Of course, it's still early in the pregnancy."

"You intend to…see the pregnancy through, then." *Mon Dieu*, but that sounded crass.

"Yes."

He allowed himself to exhale. "Good. I was hoping you would say that."

"You are?"

Given what he'd said in the past, he could understand her surprise. He was as surprised as she, really. Children—family—had never been in his plans. He'd always figured that when he grew too old to work, he would pass

D'Usay International on to some deserving person and let the name live on through the company. The more he thought about having a child, however... "Once the news sank in, and I got used to the idea..." He paused while he sipped his coffee. "I like that I will have an heir."

"You know that whether you like the idea or not doesn't really matter, right?"

"I know," he replied. "Which is why I'm glad you want this child as well."

"I see." She sat back in her chair, studying him. Philippe's skin warmed under the scrutiny. "Does that mean you're planning to be a part of this baby's life?"

"I take my responsibilities seriously. I intend to make sure he—or she—wants for nothing. I've already talked to my attorney, and he is making all the necessary arrangements."

"Financial arrangements, you mean."

"Yes. I want to make sure my child, and its mother, are well provided for," he said.

Jenna was frowning.

"What is wrong?"

"Nothing," she replied. "Go on."

He hated when women used that word. *Nothing never meant nothing.* She was upset with him, probably still angry for his being out of touch this past week. There was little he could say that would go over well until her irritation cooled. "Perhaps we should wait and have this discussion when we've both had some rest," he said. When they weren't tired and peevish. "Tonight, over dinner?" Good food, the right atmosphere. Yes, dinner was definitely a better plan.

Jenna shook her head. "I can't. I have to work."

"Not until later on. We can eat early, and then I can drive you to the nursing home."

"I…"

Acting completely on impulse, he reached across the table to clutch her hand. The first thing he noticed was how cool and damp her skin was. It reminded him of that afternoon in Arles when they'd gotten soaked to the skin. He covered hers with his second hand to warm her. "Please, Jenna. I want to do this right."

Her eyes darkened. Was she thinking of that day as well? "All right, dinner." She pulled her hand free. "But I'll drive myself."

"Very well." Why her answer bothered him, he wasn't sure, but no sooner had she mentioned driving herself than he felt a wave of frustration. "I'm staying at the Merchant Seafarer."

* * *

Naturally Philippe would stay at the Seafarer, the hotel where the adventure began. As she walked into the lobby, Jenna recalled how excited she and Shirley had been when they attended the fund-raiser. The sumptuous hotel wasn't someplace they regularly hung out, it being far too pricey for anything but special occasions.

"I guess dinner with your daddy counts as a special occasion, too," she said as she settled in amid the seascapes and whaling artifacts to wait for Philippe. Apparently talking to her stomach was going to be a thing.

The fire in the giant fireplace gave the room an old-fashioned warmth. Under different circumstances, the setting would be romantic with its candlelight and black ocean views. Two months ago, she and Philippe would have been exchanging simmering smiles from across a table. Tonight they would be discussing financial arrangements for their child.

The thought made her stomach churn. Why did his emphasis on money bother her so? Seriously, what else did she expect? The man had made his feelings about children quite clear that afternoon on the Tour Magne. As far as he was concerned, she was carrying an unexpected liability. She should be grateful he wanted to shoulder responsibility at all, and that times had changed enough that he didn't feel the need to do "the right thing."

What was it about the women in her family and accidental pregnancies, anyway? First there was her grandmother—unless her mother had been the healthiest five-month preemie ever born—then her mother, and now her. Talk about a family legacy.

"How about when you grow up, you break family tradition," she said to the baby. "Find someone who loves you back, and *then* have the baby."

When she put it like that, she sounded like she was in love with Philippe. She wasn't.

At all.

Not a bit.

At precisely six o'clock, the elevator doors opened and Philippe emerged, accompanied by a blond man who looked vaguely familiar. When he saw her sitting by the fire, he smiled. Jenna hated how her insides swooped in response. Months later and she was still reacting to him physically. Had to be hormones.

He greeted her with a kiss on the cheek. "You look beautiful."

No, she didn't. She'd worn the most staid

outfit she owned. Black slacks and a bulky gray turtleneck. She looked like she was attending a funeral.

"This is Kit Merchant," he continued, turning to his companion.

That was why the stranger looked familiar. The hotel owner had sponsored the charity auction.

"Kit and I spent a summer sailing in St. Tropez back before I took over D'Usay International. It was a fortunate coincidence that he was here this week as well."

"I understand you recently stayed at the Château de Beauchamp," Kit said after the introductions. "I hope your trip was everything you imagined."

"And then some." To Jenna's surprise, the answer rolled right off her tongue without embarrassment or awkwardness. The trip had been wonderful. It was only her carelessness that she regretted.

"Congratulations, by the way," she added. "I read in the paper that the clinic is just about complete."

"Yes, and not a minute too soon, what with cold weather coming. Beating an addiction is hard enough without the added pressure of finding a safe place to stay. This clinic will help a lot of people."

"That's wonderful."

"I wish I could do more. The islands have as big a problem as the rest of the Cape."

"It's a good start."

"You're right, and if we're lucky, we'll help spare a family the torture of losing a loved one to the streets."

As he finished, his eyes took on a faraway look. This wasn't mere generosity on his part; it was personal. At the auction, someone said Kit lost a friend to an overdose. Clearly the story was true.

"And," he added, "thanks to Philippe, we'll be able to provide some of the extras we had to strike from the budget."

Philippe had made a donation?

"It was the least I could do," the Frenchman replied. "Matt was a good guy."

"It's still greatly appreciated," Kit said. "If there's anything I can do in return, let me know. It was good seeing you again, my friend. Ms. Brown, I hope you won't be a stranger."

"That was very generous of you to make a donation," Jenna said once Kit departed.

Again Philippe shrugged. "The three of us, Kit, Matt, and I, enjoyed some good times together. Matt was a hell of a sailor as well. I had heard rumors he was battling something, but I didn't know how bad things had gotten."

And he knew as well as anyone how it felt to lose someone close to you. In her annoyance over his comments this morning, she'd forgotten that part of him. "Opioid addiction is insidious. It can take hold before you realize, and breaking free is a hard battle. I have seen more than one nurse fall prey after an injury at work. Goes to show, addiction can affect anyone, no matter the background."

"Let us pray then that neither of us ever have to watch a friend battle the disease." Philippe squeezed her hand. The soft understanding in his eyes made Jenna's heart clench. *This* was the Philippe she remembered from her trip. The one who made her feel understood.

"And that Kit's clinic makes a difference," she said.

"*Oui.* Let us hope."

Neither of them made a motion to let go. From the corner of her eye, Jenna caught his arm lifting upward, to tangle in her curls the way he loved to do before kissing her. Her pulse quickened. Was he going to kiss her now?

The hand pulled back, and just like that,

the moment vanished. "Ready for dinner?" he asked.

The heaviness in her stomach was annoyance, not disappointment. "Sure," she said. Might as well get the financial arrangements settled.

Kit had arranged for them to have a table by the corner window, tucked away from the other diners. An ice bucket was already in place, the bottle chilled and ready to be opened. Just like that first night on the terrace, she thought wryly. How appropriate.

"Sparkling cider," Philippe told her. "I've never had it myself, but I thought it bad form to drink in front of you."

"I wouldn't have minded."

"I would have. Besides, how can we toast unless you have a glass as well?"

"What do we possibly have to toast?" she asked.

"Many things," he replied. "The *bébé* for one."

"I'll give you that." The baby was definitely worthy of a toast.

As they touched the rims of their glasses, their eyes connected. Two months hadn't diminished the magnetism of Philippe's eyes. They were as deep and vivid as ever. Maybe because there were no lavender fields to invite comparison. Only cold dark water and gray October sky. Jenna loved color. In France, brightness had been everywhere.

Or was her memory being misled by the eyes across the table? The fields would be barren now. Bright never lasted.

"Did you finish your harvest on time?" she asked him.

"Pardon?"

"You were worried the harvesters would fall behind schedule when I left France. Did they get everything cut and distilled on time?" Her question had caught him off guard. She asked because she wasn't ready to talk finances yet, and the farm was the first topic that came to mind.

"We did," he answered. "In the end, it was a good harvest. The jasmine did particularly well. We managed to produce a surplus of jasmine oil."

"Congratulations." She was wearing the jasmine perfume he'd bought her and wondered if he'd noticed when he kissed her hello. Although whether he did or not didn't really matter.

"What comes now?"

"Are you referring to the company? Or for…"

"The company." She still wasn't ready for baby finances.

"We start working on securing contracts for the next year or so and focus on the crops growing in our other locales." He took a sip of cider. "That is why I was in the UK. Colliers of London is interested in our lilies."

"The soap company?"

Philippe nodded. "They are one of the few large companies left who prefer natural to synthetic materials."

"Does that mean we should toast congratulations?"

"It's too premature for toasts, I'm afraid," he said. "We're still in the negotiation phase."

"That makes sense. You don't want to celebrate until you are absolutely sure."

"Exactly."

Having milked the topic as much as possible, they fell silent. Jenna filled the space by pretending to study the menu. Peering over the edge, she saw Philippe running his fingers up and down the stem of his glass. It was the first time she'd ever seen him do anything that could be considered fidgeting. "About this morning," he began. "I am sorry I didn't warn you of my arrival. I didn't mean to put you off balance."

"Thank you." Even though they'd covered his regret this morning, she appreciated the direct apology. As an olive branch of her own, she teased, "I thought maybe it was your passive-aggressive way of getting back for putting you off balance with my call."

He smiled. "I'll never tell."

Once again, they grew silent, the elephant in the room making civil conversation impossible until it was acknowledged. "I'm sorry," she said. "I know the situation—"

"Don't." He cut her off. "It was my eagerness that got us here."

"We were both eager, if you recall."

"Indeed I do." The candlelight flickered in the dark of his eyes, and for a second they were back in France. Jenna's cheeks warmed the way they did whenever she pictured them together. Remembering how Philippe's touches flipped a switch inside her, causing everything else to fade away.

"Regardless of how…" The sound of his voice brought reality back. "It's important you know I have every intention of meeting my responsibilities as a parent."

So much for avoiding the elephant. "You said as much this morning," she replied. He'd even used the same word. *Responsibility.* She felt a sting in her midsection, although she wasn't sure why. *Responsibility* was a perfectly good word. An accurate word. "You...you said you talked to your lawyer?"

"I asked him to establish a trust in the child's name with you as trustee. Whatever happens to me or D'Usay International, the child won't suffer."

"You envision something happening?"

"I believe in planning for contingencies. Nothing lasts forever, especially in a world where technology is quickly replacing tradition. For all I know, D'Usay International will fade long before I do. I want to make sure my son's future is secure."

The word *son* didn't escape her. "You're hoping for a boy. To carry on the d'Usay name."

"Are you surprised?"

"Not really." Given his attachment to family history, she expected nothing less.

"I'm glad you understand," he said, reaching for his glass. "Seeing the name continued is important to me. In fact..."

Their conversation was cut short by the arrival of the waitress to read the evening specials. A tall blonde, she had breasts as perfect as naval oranges and wore a pencil skirt so narrow that Jenna was surprised she could walk.

Launching into a detailed description of the catch of the day, the woman kept her attention squarely on Philippe. Jenna might not have existed. To his credit, Philippe kept his charm dialed back to seven out of ten, smiling with charm, but not overtly so as he listened.

"I hope I'm not cramping your style," she said once the waitress walked away. Slowly, Jenna might add, and with a whole lot of hip action.

God, that sounded jealous and petty. She drowned the thought with a gulp of ice water.

Philippe gave her an odd look. "Are you talking about the waitress?"

"She's very pretty, and obviously interested." Her second sentence came out moderately less shrewish.

"I'm here to discuss our child, not to pick up waitresses. Would think you'd give me a little credit."

"I'm sorry. I didn't mean to insult you. It's just that I know I don't…never mind." The fact she didn't have any claim on his dating life didn't require saying.

How many women had shared his bed since her departure? She didn't want know and yet at the same time had a perverse curiosity. She had a feeling the answer would depress her.

"You were about to say something before the waitress arrived," she said. "We were talking about the baby having your last name."

"Right." Suddenly he was back to twisting the glass stem. "I was about to say that I'd like the child to carry my name whether it is a boy or a girl."

"Okay."

"Unfortunately, my lawyer informs me I don't have control over the matter. Since we are not married, you are free to give the child your last name if you prefer, even if I acknowledge paternity."

Was this why he was fidgeting with the glass? Because he thought she might refuse his request? "I don't really know the law regarding baby names, but I just said I was okay with the child having your name."

"But you could change your mind."

"Are you suggesting I would renege on a promise like that?" Now she was the one insulted. "I know how important your family legacy is to you. What do you think I'm going to do, threaten to name the baby Brown as some kind of bargaining chip?"

Philippe looked down at his place setting. "Xavier…"

"Xavier what?"

"Hasn't had the pleasure of knowing you as well as I do," he replied. "As a result, he's being overprotective."

Underneath the table, Jenna balled her hand into a fist. She tried to see the situation from Philippe's perspective. All the attorney knew was that she was a pregnant American. He was paid to be mistrustful.

Philippe, on the other hand. They'd shared a bed. Bared their souls. "I would never be that petty or vindictive."

"I know."

His right hand disappeared from the tabletop. A second later, Jenna felt his grip surrounding her fingers. "I know," he repeated softly. There was nothing but sincerity in his expression.

The warmth from his touch spread up her arm and into her chest. "So, what kind of legal assurances does Xavier want?"

"Well…" He took a deep breath. "Xavier outlined a couple of possibilities. One is to make my last name a stipulation of the trust."

"In other words, sign something that says I don't get access to the funds unless the baby carries your name."

"Exactly."

Sounded crass when said out loud, as if the

money was the sole factor. She never wanted their child to think he or she was a cash cow.

"And the other option?" she asked. "You said there were a couple."

"Yes, we…"

Jenna had forgotten they were holding hands beneath the table until his grasp grew tighter. Philippe's expression had grown serious, too, making the hair on the back of her neck start to prickle.

"We could get married," he said.

CHAPTER SEVEN

JENNA'S JAW DROPPED. Marry him? That was the next suggestion? Mr. Marriage and Family Require Too Much of a Commitment?

"Don't dismiss the idea out of hand," he said, gripping her hand tighter. "If you are my wife, the child carries my name."

"So would I," she pointed out. Surely the attorney had noted that she came with the deal.

"Only for a short while. We need only stay married long enough for the baby to be born. Then we can dissolve our agreement."

"Not dissolve, divorce," she corrected. Semantics, maybe, but the word mattered. Marriage wasn't the same as an agreement to grow flowers.

"Very well, we will divorce once the baby is born."

Jenna took a deep breath. "Tell your lawyer I'll sign any kind of stipulation he wants," she said.

Philippe frowned. In his confusion, Jenna pulled her hand free but kept it under the table. She didn't want him to see how much she was trembling. How could he make such a suggestion? Was he not listening when she talked about her parents?

"I do not understand," he said. "I am offering…"

"To do the right thing. Yes, I know." That added to the suggestion's sting. Philippe believed he was doing the right thing.

"My father did the right thing, too. So did my grandfather. And, while I appreciate your dedication to family traditions, I'd prefer not to repeat mine." Mentally, she gave herself a pat on the back for speaking calmly.

He shook his head. "But this would be different," he said.

"How? I'm pregnant, you're suggesting marriage." Where was there a difference? "Seems the same to me."

"Except that both of us would be entering the marriage with the same expectations."

In other words, their marriage would be different because there was no expectation of it being real. Jenna had to give him credit. He was honest.

What surprised her was to hear him press the issue. Was it an ego thing—shock that someone would say no—or was it because he wanted the baby born in wedlock? Either way, there was one very key ingredient missing. No way she was marrying anyone who didn't love her. She, and her baby, deserved better.

"Doesn't matter. The answer is still no."

"Are you sure?"

"Positive. Have your lawyer draw up whatever papers he wants." She looked to her glass, not wanting to see the relief that was no doubt in his eyes.

Or for him to see the disappointment that was in hers.

That could have gone better. Philippe ordered a brandy before settling into the shadows of a leather bench seat. Jenna and he had said their goodbyes a few minutes earlier. A very polite hug outside the front doors, barely long enough for him to register the lines of her body, before she slipped into her waiting car. As soon as her taillights disappeared into the night, he'd headed for the hotel bar.

Fortunately, the place was deserted except

for the bartender, who was more interested in the American football game on the television set. His disinterest allowed Philippe the privacy to recount the night's events.

Had he thought honestly Jenna would consider his proposal? He knew her story—part of it, at least. But their situation was different, was it not? Besides, he wasn't offering permanence; she could leave whenever she wanted.

But apparently she preferred to sign a legal document instead. Fine. He should be relieved the situation would be resolved so civilly. He'd dodged a bullet, as it were. There were plenty of women in his past that wouldn't have been so understanding.

"You lost your friend."

It was the waitress from the restaurant. She set his brandy on the table before angling her head toward the bartender. "He's more interested in seeing if New England scores on this drive, so I volunteered to bring your order. I'm surprised to see you alone."

"She had to go to work," Philippe replied.

"Too bad. Would you like some company?"

He studied the woman over his drink. She was quite lovely, and from the gleam in her eye, she was the kind of woman who wasn't looking for anything beyond a good night. Just his type.

The image of cinnamon curls splayed across his pillow popped into his head.

"Perhaps another time. I have a lot on my mind tonight," he told the waitress.

The waitress shrugged, disappointed, but not too. "Signal if you need anything."

She swayed back to the bar, leaving Philippe alone to sip his drink.

And wonder why he hadn't accepted a woman's invitation since Jenna left France.

Jenna had just enough time to change into her uniform and report for her shift. When she stepped off the elevator, Shirley was waiting for her at the nurses' station.

"We've got five minutes," her friend said. "How'd it go?"

"Dinner? Fine. I had the chicken *amandine*. We toasted the baby's good health. Oh, and he proposed."

"He what?"

"Keep your voice down!" Jenna whispered harshly. "I don't need the whole floor knowing." She looked out on to the floor to see if anyone was listening, but their colleagues had their heads hunched over the computers, updating patient information. "He suggested that we get married."

Once she finished explaining the whole story, her friend sank into a nearby chair. "Wow, he doesn't mess around, does he? From the way you described him, I never would have pegged him for the traditional type. Did you…?"

"He only proposed out of obligation."

"You sound disappointed," Shirley said.

"Don't be ridiculous." Why would she be disappointed? Wasn't as though she was in love with Philippe d'Usay. What they shared in France—the connection, the intimacy—were emotions of the moment. Trying to extend them was a pipe dream. She wasn't about to compound reckless behavior with more reckless behavior.

"I have absolutely zero interest in marrying Philippe. Why would I want to be my mother?"

"Trapped in a never-ending codependent relationship with a narcissist?" Shirley asked.

"I meant tying myself to someone who doesn't love me."

"Only in this case the tie would be temporary and you don't love him. Right?" Shirley held up a hand. "Relax, I'm yanking your chain. You totally made the right call."

"Thank you."

A glance at the clock said the shift was about to start. Jenna headed into the tiny room behind the nurses' station to lock up her pocket-book. As she shoved it into one of the lockers that lined the back wall, she heard her phone start to buzz. Whoever it was would have to wait. Patients came first.

"I hate to start the shift on a down note," said Donna, one of the nurses on the eleven-to-seven shift, "but Mr. Mylanski isn't doing so good." She relayed the older man's vitals. "You might want to call his family and give them the heads-up."

The news cast a pall on the atmosphere. Shirley swore. "I thought he'd have a little longer. Poor guy. I'll call his daughter."

"And, on the opposite end of the spectrum," their colleague continued, "Lola has been restless all night." Lola being one of their patients with dementia. "She keeps sneaking out of her room and climbing into other patients' beds."

"I'll keep an eye on her," Jenna volunteered. Chasing after Lola would keep her too busy to think about Philippe. At least for a few hours.

Eight long hours later, an exhausted Jenna stepped out into the early-morning sunshine.

"I don't know about you, but I could use breakfast," she said to Shirley. "I forgot my sweet cheese croissant and baby's annoyed. Wanna join me? My treat." Mr. Mylanski had passed an hour before, and she figured her friend could use the distraction.

Shirley shook her head. "Thanks, but I'm going to go home and take a hot bath."

"You sure?" Wasn't like Shirley to give up free food. The phone in Jenna's bag was buzzing again. She wasn't in the mood to take the call now anymore than she was any of the other times during her shift. "Did you miss the part where I said my treat?"

"Positive," Shirley replied. "Besides, I think you already have plans." She nodded to the parking lot, where Philippe was walking their way.

"What's he doing here?" Jenna asked.

"Beats me. You'll have to ask him," Shirley replied.

He'd gone casual, in jeans and a black sweater that emphasized his shoulders and muscular arms. When he saw Jenna he smiled.

Jenna's stomach swooped, and it wasn't morning sickness.

"*Bonjour*, ladies," he greeted. "The time difference had me up early, so I thought I would bring you breakfast." In his hand he carried a tray of cups and a white paper sack. He handed one of the cups to Shirley. "This is for you. I am afraid I don't know how you prefer it."

"Free works," Shirley replied, "but if you have sugar, I won't say no."

"Sugar packets are in the bag, along with one of those sweet cheese pastries you said helped with the morning sickness." He looked back and forth between her and Jenna. Shirley had dark circles from the night's stress; Jenna guessed she looked the same. "Is everything all right?" he asked.

"We lost a patient last night," Jenna explained.

"I'm sorry."

"Thank you. He was a sweet old man," Shirley said. "I'll miss him."

"At least his family made it in time to say goodbye," Jenna said.

"Yes, that is good. No one should die alone." Philippe frowned, leaving her to wonder if he was referring to more than Mr. Mylanski.

"Is this a bad time?" he asked.

"Not for me," Shirley replied. "I've got a date with a hot tub."

"Jenna?"

Jenna eyed the white paper sack he held.

Baby really needed to eat. She couldn't believe he'd remembered she said the baby craved sweet cheese croissants.

"There's a park a short way from the coffee shop we visited yesterday. If you don't mind eating on a bench, we can go there. This hour of the day we'll have privacy."

"A park bench is fine. Lead the way."

Jenna waited until they'd walked a few paces before accepting the drink. Warm water with honey and lemon. Same order as the day before. She tried not to be touched that he remembered.

"I didn't think I'd see you today," she said.

"Why not?"

"Because…" Because they'd said everything they had to say last night. With his business complete, what reason would he have to stay? "Is this about the paperwork you wanted me to sign?"

"Xavier is fast, but not that fast," he replied.

"Then…?"

"Perhaps I wanted to enjoy your company. We are having a child together. Shouldn't we be friendly? What is that buzzing sound?"

Jenna sighed. "It's my phone." The vibration could be heard coming from her pocketbook.

"Do you need to answer?"

"Definitely not." It was way too early for drama, just like last night had been too late. "They'll leave a message." Or call back again, more likely. "I'm not talking to anyone until I've had my pastry."

"Present company excluded, I hope."

"Only because you brought the pastry," she replied. "Although there's no guarantee I won't be too busy soothing my stomach to talk with you, either."

Because of the hour, the park was empty except for a lone dog walker. In the center, there was a bench overlooking the walking paths. Using his handkerchief, Philippe wiped away the moisture and fallen leaves and they took a seat.

The moment was surprisingly peaceful. After a long, crazy night, it was pleasant to simply sit and listen to the sounds of the birds waking in the bushes. Philippe had stretched his arm along the back of the bench, a warm, protective barrier against Jenna's shoulders.

"Reminds me of the morning we had breakfast at Marguerite's," he remarked.

"Except the weather was warmer and we were on a busy street corner surrounded by people instead of sitting under an oak tree,"

Jenna said once she'd washed down the last of her croissant. "Other than that, though."

"Completely the same."

They both chuckled. Jenna knew exactly what Philippe meant.

That morning had felt peaceful, too. The silence between them easy.

He nodded and sipped his coffee. "I'm sorry about your patient."

"Thanks. He'd only been with us a couple months, but we all liked him. I feel bad for his family. No one likes losing a loved one."

"No, they do not."

Jenna winced. Fatigue was making her insensitive. She touched his knee in apology, earning a slight smile in return.

"You said his family was there, correct? He did not die alone?"

He wouldn't have died alone regardless— Shirley would have made a point of sitting with him—but something in the way Philippe was double-checking about Mr. Mylanski's family said the point mattered to him.

"All but one son," she told him. "He lives in Boston and couldn't get across until this morning."

"Too late," he murmured. "He must feel terrible."

He looked out over the grass, his profile as open as Jenna had ever seen, excepting that afternoon in his apartment. "I wasn't with either of my parents when they died. No one told me until after the fact. With Felix... I tried, but I couldn't get there in time. I was in Italy, and by the time I saw the hospital had called and arranged a flight... He died all alone."

In that moment, his comments from before made sense. Mr. Mylanski's death must have triggered his guilt. Armchair analysis wasn't what he needed right now, though. She sat back and waited for him to continue.

"I thought I had more time. I wanted to make this one last deal before... So he'd know he was leaving the business in good hands. If I had known the end was close, I would have..."

"Canceled your trip?" she asked. "Do you think that's what your brother would have wanted? For you to let the business languish while you sat vigil twenty-four-seven?"

Tucking a leg beneath her, she turned to face him, her hand squeezing his knee. "You were doing what your brother wanted you to do—you were taking care of the business."

"How do you know what he wanted?" he asked.

Oh, why did his eyes have to be so sad? "I don't know for certain," she told him. "But you told me your brother loved the business."

"More than loved. He was born to run D'Usay International."

"And did he want you to be as dedicated to the company as he was?" Philippe nodded. "Then he would have wanted you to be spending your time making the business grow..."

She cupped his cheek and looked him straight in the eye as she told him the same words she'd told others over her career. Only this time, they felt far more important. "You tried your best, Philippe. That's all you could do. Your brother knows that."

"*Merci*," he whispered, eyes shining. He leaned briefly into her touch before kissing her palm and backing away. "Listen to me. You lost a patient and I'm making the moment about myself."

"Don't apologize. I like when you open up." Knowing he trusted her enough to reveal even the slightest vulnerability touched her more than any compliment. "You don't have to be charming and witty all the time."

"But I am so good at being charming and witty." His eyes sparkled for a moment before returning to the dark violet they were before. "You make it easy," he said. "To share the thoughts in my head. I don't know why, but you do."

"Not at first," Jenna reminded him. "Remember I had to push?"

"And now look at me. You've created a morbid monster."

"Morbid? Maybe. Monster? Far from it."

His eyes locked with hers. Piece by piece, the noise around them died away until all Jenna could hear was the pulse fluttering in her throat. She wasn't even sure she was breathing.

"Thank you for listening." Philippe was whispering. Was he afraid to break the silence, too?

"Anytime," she whispered back.

His gaze dropped to her mouth, his eyes dark and heavy-lidded. Jenna's gaze hitched. She knew that look. She felt her body start to lean toward his, the way metal moved toward a magnet.

"I want to see you tonight," he whispered. "Will you have dinner with me?"

"I don't know." When he looked at her like that, she had trouble thinking clearly. Was this entire conversation to break down her defenses and revisit what they shared in Provence, or was he attempting to be friendly with the mother of his child? She was too confused to know.

"I've never been to Nantucket," he was saying. "I'd like to see your island."

Her island. He knew the right phrases to melt her resistance. Pulling her eyes away she studied the dents in her drink lid, hoping the answers lay in the white plastic.

"All right." The answer came out automatically. "I'll show you around Nantucket. You might as well know about where your child is going to grow up."

Out of the corner of her eye, she thought she saw Philippe shooting her a look. Apparently he hadn't considered the baby would live on Nantucket.

"But first, I need to go to bed. To sleep," she quickly added. "We can take your tour later this afternoon."

"Very good. I will call you to work out a time." His expression brightened, and Jenna immediately felt her insides take a tumble. Damn if he couldn't obliterate her resolve with a single smile. "I'm looking forward to it."

Heaven help her, so was she.

CHAPTER EIGHT

Philippe stared at the string of messages in his in-box. Xavier was on him to go over the contracts for the upcoming year. There were changes in the terms that the lawyer wanted to review with him. The growers in Belgium were making noises about a potential work stoppage over wages. If they succeeded, it would start a chain reaction eastward to Asia. Dozens of little fires demanded his attention, and here he was thinking of ways to extend his stay in Nantucket.

Truth be told, he could have departed that morning, but when his alarm went off, he found himself unwilling to leave. Normally he couldn't wait to be on his way home. Then again, normally he grew tired of a woman's company by this point in their relationship as well. Instead, he looked forward to see-ing Jenna as much that afternoon as he had that first day in France. Every time he tried to work, his brain went to her sitting on the bench in the sunshine. He'd thought of her all night, too, her soft, pale skin invading his dreams.

Of course her dominating his thoughts could be easily explained. She was carrying his child. It was only natural that she—and her well-being—should be on his mind.

Only it isn't her well-being you're thinking about, it's her.

Once again, Jenna Brown was proving the exception to his rules.

Like the strange ability she had to make him share his feelings.

Until today, he'd never told a soul how guilty he felt at not being by Felix's bedside when he died. His only chance to actually say goodbye, and he'd failed.

Strangely enough though, he felt better for talking. Jenna hadn't said anything profound, but she'd still managed to comfort him. Small wonder he nearly kissed her.

Leaning back in his chair, he relived those moments on the bench, rewriting them so that he tasted her kiss. Been too long, he thought. Far too long. He missed her.

Shortly before three thirty, Philippe pulled up in front of Jenna's address. Immediately, he knew which side of the duplex was hers. The one with the tricolor corn hanging on the door wreath and potted cabbages lining the porch steps.

As he stepped out of his car, he spied Jenna through a first-floor window talking on the phone. Whoever was on the other end was making her tense. She was pacing in and out of view and rubbing the back of her neck.

She was still tense when she answered his knock, her pink lips drawn in a tight line. "Is everything all right?" he asked.

"I need to learn not to answer the phone on the way out," she replied. "Someone always needs something when you're rushing to get ready."

Her face held the same taut expression as this morning when she'd refused to answer the phone in her bag. His guess? Whoever she'd been avoiding had finally connected with her, and she wasn't happy.

"If you have business, I don't mind waiting," he told her.

"Not necessary. I'm done with them." She stepped outside and shut the door. Not before Philippe caught a glimpse of a brightly painted entrance way, however. "Besides, we only have

a couple hours of daylight. If you want to sight-
see, we shouldn't dawdle."

"Good point," he replied. Although was her
rush really about daylight?

"I'm looking forward to seeing your island,"
he said as they walked down her steps.

"I wish you wouldn't call it my island. I
don't even own the house I live in."

"You live here though, no? Experience all
the seasons? Then it is your island," he added
once she'd nodded her answer. He opened the
passenger door and waited while she slid in
and buckled her seat belt. "And I am looking
forward to taking a tour."

"As long as you don't expect a detailed history lesson along with it."

"I believe we've already established your
historical illiteracy." His teasing comment
barely elicited a smile. The phone call had definitely dampened her mood. At least he hoped
it was the phone call. "Where to first?"

"Main Street."

They spent the next hour or so walking the
winding cobblestoned streets. Little by little
Jenna's mood seemed to lift, and soon she was
pointing out landmarks and sharing anecdotes
with a smile. True to her warning, she didn't
provide much enlightenment in the way of

local history, but she did provide a glimpse into her life, which Philippe found just as enlightening. Listening to her wax enthusiastically about the fried clams and lobster rolls served at the various restaurants, he learned that her dining tastes were simple and unpretentious. Her anecdote about the pets on parade during the local Christmas walk told him she had a fondness for animals. And her soft gaze at a little boy buying a stuffed black dog from one of the stores said she was looking forward to having their child. It was, perhaps, better than any history lesson.

They moved from Main Street to the south. "From what I'm told, this street used to be called Prison Street," Jenna told him.

"Why is that?"

"Going out on a limb, I'd say because there was a prison." He cast her a look. "Seriously. They're restoring the old jail about a half mile down. No doubt that's what inspired the name."

"Logical." Saltbox houses from the eighteenth century lined both sides of the road. Philippe found their brown and gray shuttered shapes quaint. One particular house had a tall tower in its backyard, a strangely modern-looking structure. "Is that an observatory?" he asked.

"Yep. On weekends they open it up so you can see the stars."

"Odd that would be stuck in a row of antique homes."

"Not really. The woman who lived in that particular house was an astronomer. One of the first female astronomers in the country, in fact."

"You don't say." Philippe craned his neck to look upward. "Too bad it is not yet dark—we could go look at the stars ourselves."

"Closed for the season," she told him. "Plus, I already climbed one narrow tower with you. I'm not climbing a second."

"Chicken." The remark earned him a nudge from her shoulder—the first contact of the evening. Instantly Philippe wanted to touch her in return, but he held back, stuffing his hands in his back pockets instead.

"I didn't appreciate how much of your island closes up during the winter," he said.

"Only the parts that cater to the tourists and summer residents. There are plenty of year-round businesses to keep the economy flowing in the off-season."

"Nevertheless, so many people leave when the weather turns cold. It must get very cold and lonely."

"Cold, definitely. Nantucket nor'easters can be pretty brutal."

Philippe wasn't sure what a nor'easter was, but he understood the word *brutal*. If he counted correctly, Jenna would be well into her second trimester during those brutal months. When ice and snow could make a person lose their balance.

A wave of unease washed over him. "Perhaps you should consider staying off the island during those months, and go somewhere a little less stormy."

"No need." She waved off his concern. "I've been here a couple of years now, and it's not so bad. You learn to deal with the weather."

"You weren't pregnant those winters."

"No, but… Oh, I get what you're saying now." She stopped walking so she could face him. "I hate to break it to you, but people have babies on Nantucket all the time, winter included."

But they weren't having *his* baby. Philippe was only concerned with her. "What if you slip on ice and fall during one of these nor'easters you talked about?"

"I could slip and fall anywhere," she replied. "Conditions don't have to be icy for a person to lose their balance. I'll be fine." She started walking again.

Fine. Philippe had heard that word before. He didn't want Jenna to be fine. He wanted her—and their baby—safe.

"It isn't as if you will need to work during the pregnancy," he called after her. "You would be free to go and do whatever you wanted." Except fall.

"Philippe." Again she stopped, only this time when she turned, she had her arms crossed. "Are you planning to make my getting off the island one of the trust stipulations?"

"No."

"Then back off, okay? I'm a grown woman. I don't need you mother-henning me into moving."

"I'm not trying to make you move," he said. "I'm simply trying to keep the baby safe."

"Well, you'll have to trust me."

"I'll try." The knot in his chest made it difficult.

"Try hard." Spinning on her heel, she resumed walking, her pace quick enough that he had to pick up speed to catch up.

"Do you mind if I ask you a question?" he asked after a quarter mile of silence. He didn't want to contribute to the chill between them any more than he already had, but he was curious. "What made you choose here to live? A single woman like yourself, I would think Boston would be far more appealing."

To his relief, she took the question for the peace offering he meant it to be. "I lived in Boston for a year or two after graduation. Decided I'd rather be three hours away."

He was about to ask why when her pocketbook began buzzing. The woman had the loudest vibration setting he had ever heard. "Your phone is ringing."

"I'm sorry. I probably should answer. Only because the nursing home might be looking for shift coverage." Unzipping her bag, she reached in and pulled out her cell phone. "I'll let them know...never mind." Her expression fell. "It's not the home after all."

She dropped the phone into her bag unanswered.

"You still could have talked with them," Philippe said.

"Could have, but I don't want to," she replied. He noticed the way the muscles in her jaw twitched from it being clenched. Her tension had returned. Was it the same caller as before? The one she had spent the morning avoiding as well? He was trying his best not to pry, but watching Jenna turn from smiling to angry in the blink of an eye had him suddenly quite upset with the person as well—whoever that person might be.

A thought struck him. "You are not being bothered by someone, are you? A former lover, perhaps?"

"Good Lord, no." Her laugh had a mocking tone. "More like the opposite."

"A current lover." He was definitely angry.

"Try my mother."

Ah, the woman who couldn't move on from Jenna's father. Why didn't she want to speak with her? He ventured a semi guess. "You are mad at her?"

"Frustrated," Jenna replied. "It's just more of the same, and I've got enough on my plate without piling on more drama. Honest to God, sometimes I don't understand what's going on in her head. Do you know what I mean?"

"I take it she is making decisions you don't approve of."

"I'm not really in a position to judge other people's behavior, am I?" She pressed a palm to her stomach. "But, yeah, I think… Check that. She is making a big mistake."

"Are you sure? Perhaps you don't know the whole story." Much like how he felt right now.

He was playing devil's advocate because saying *I'm sorry* seemed trite and he didn't know what else to say.

"Oh, I know the whole story, all right," Jenna replied. "This isn't the first time we've been through this drama."

This time he did apologize, for the stress the call was obviously causing. Both Jenna's jaw and her fist were clenched. Such tension couldn't be good for the baby. He looked around for a place where they could sit and talk in earnest, saw mostly trees and weathered picket fences. There was, however, a small historical center across the street from the observatory that had a tall set of steps leading to its porch. He motioned for Jenna to follow him over. If anyone balked, he'd pay the membership fee.

"Why?" she asked.

"So you can relax," he said. "Your shoulders look ready to snap."

"Sorry. I just get so…"

"Frustrated. You said as much." He waited until she'd taken a seat on one of the steps before positioning himself behind her and placing his hands on her shoulders. Naturally, as soon as he touched her, the muscles tightened even more. Philippe kneaded the tension. Over the years, countless women had told him he had talented hands. Now was a good time to put the compliments to the test.

"Perhaps you would feel better if you told me what was going on," he told her.

"I can't," she replied. "It's too... God, that feels good."

He pressed his thumbs against muscle. "Your shoulders are in knots."

"That's because every time I think about it, I want to scream. How can someone, in this day and age, be as clueless as my mother? I know what's going to happen, too. I'm going to have to pick up the pieces."

Pieces of her mother? "I'm sorry," he said. "I'm confused."

"I know you are. I don't mean to be cryptic." Heaving a deep sigh, she closed her eyes. Philippe would have liked to say it was because she enjoyed the massage, but the look on her face suggested it was out of embarrassment.

"My father's back."

Saying the words out loud only made her feel more frustrated. She felt Philippe's hands still for a moment before continuing their ministrations. Under other circumstances, the massage would feel heavenly.

"Your parents are having an affair."

"Yep." And not for the first time, either. "Dad's current relationship is on the rocks— that can happen when you sleep with the new inventory manager at work—and he needed a friendly shoulder. Naturally…"

"He turned to your mother."

And like always, her mother was ready, willing and able to give him all the compassion he desired. "They've been 'involved' for a couple weeks," she told him.

"Perhaps this time they will…"

"No, they won't." While she appreciated his attempt to be positive, she'd seen this situation too many times before. Her father coming back all smiles and sweetness, telling her mother everything she wanted to hear. "This is the same thing he always does," she said. "They'll be together two, three weeks, until someone else catches his eye. Mom's his emotional comfort food."

"And your mother, she lets him treat her this way?" Jenna could tell he found the idea as unfathomable as she did.

"Every single time. Dad can be quite the charmer when he wants to be."

Like someone else Jenna knew. Although unlike her father, Philippe managed expectations. You knew what you were—or weren't—getting with Philippe. Her father promised love and forever.

She allowed her head to fall forward as Philippe's fingers slid upward along either side of her spine toward her neck. "Naturally my mom's over the moon. She spent ten minutes talking about the two dozen roses he sent to her office."

"Roses are the lazy man's flower."

Jenna couldn't help but smile. Of course he'd say something like that.

"I wish you could have heard her on the phone. Going on and on about how this time was different. That she always knew they'd get back together."

"He's changed, Jenna. He realizes now what's important, and that's a home with someone who loves him."

"He had that, Mom, with what's-her-name. He cheated on her."

"Because he was so unhappy. He hasn't truly been happy since we divorced."

"She must love your father very much to keep forgiving him."

"Love? Try worship. All he has to do is

crook his finger, and she comes running. It's sad."

"Surely he loves her somewhat as well." Jenna looked up to see his serious expression looking down at her. "He keeps returning to her. Comfort food or no."

"If he loved her, he'd let her move on," she replied. For a man who eschewed emotional commitment, he sounded oddly romantic. She blamed it on his having grown up with parents who loved one another.

"The worst part is the fallout *after* he moves on. Last time she went to bed and cried for a week." She sighed. "I just wish she'd show some pride and tell him to get lost."

"She can't. She loves him. What is that old phrase? You can't control what the heart wants?"

"The heart can want whatever it likes," she replied. "Doesn't mean you stop listening to your head."

Her mother was never going to change. Jenna was going to spend the rest of her life watching her have her heart broken. "It's like watching someone driving a car you know is going to explode. You warn them and warn them, and they insist on driving anyway."

"All you can do is hope they aren't too badly burned."

She lifted her head so she could look at Philippe. "Very wise words, Monsieur d'Usay."

"I have my moments." Returning her smile, he returned to working on her shoulders. His fingers were magical—although Jenna already knew that. This was different from lovemaking, however. His hands were doing more than massaging. They were bringing calm with every tense muscle he smoothed away.

"You are right about one thing," she heard him say as he pressed the base of her neck. "People would be far better off if they led with their head."

"There would certainly be a lot less heartache in this world if they did," Jenna agreed.

"Unfortunately, not everyone is as wise as we are. Do you feel better?"

"Yeah, I do." She wouldn't have thought it possible. Normally she would keep her mother's drama to herself. At most, she shared with Shirley, but since her friend tended to get angry on her behalf, Jenna usually left those conversations as ratcheted up as when she began. Talking with Philippe was different. Whenever they spoke honestly, it was as though they were on the same page in terms of emotion. They understood one another. There was a connection.

Careful, Jenna. These kinds of thoughts were what had led her into Philippe's bed.

Not to mention sounding dangerously close to something her mother would say.

"Are you sure?" Philippe asked. "Your shoulders tensed again."

"From hunger." She twisted out of his touch. So she could face him—no other reason. "How about I treat you to some true New England clam chowder? We'll see if your bouillabaisse can compete."

"And if I'm not impressed, do I get to pick dessert?"

With those dimples of his, she'd swear the man could make the simplest question sound like an innuendo. "Sure," she replied. "As long as it's ice cream. Baby needs lots of calcium."

Not to mention that, innuendo or not, she had zero intentions of letting the evening be anything more than platonic. She'd already decided as much before, but she was doubly resolved after their conversation. Taking her own advice, she was listening to her head.

And not to whatever it was she could feel swirling around her heart.

* * *

A short while later, they were driving south, stomachs warm and full. "How do you say 'I told you so' in French?" Jenna asked.

"Je te l'avais dit."

"Then *je te l'avais dit*," she replied. Someone had eaten their soup like it was their last meal. "Better than bouillabaisse, no?"

"Apples and oranges, *ma chérie*, but since thinking so makes you smile, I won't argue."

"Can't argue with someone who's right," she shot back with a laugh.

The day wasn't supposed to be this lovely. It was like they were back in France, free and easy, again. Leaning against the passenger door, Jenna studied Philippe's profile. His hair was mussed from walking in the wind, the brown waves making him look every inch the carefree playboy. She knew better, though. She knew that beneath the facade dwelled a very complex man who mourned his family and respected the past. She loved when he dropped his mask around her. Those moments were a gift that made her feel incredibly special. In those times, it was easy to pretend theirs was a bond unlike his other relationships.

"You want to turn by that street sign," she told him.

They were headed to Madaket. Taking in the unobstructed sunset from the beach was something every visitor to the island had to experience. "The view will rival your lavender fields," she told him.

"Never, but again I am willing to indulge. As I said, I like your smile."

Jenna's cheeks warmed. "I'm looking forward to seeing the sunset myself. Believe it or not, I haven't been out this way in ages."

"Is that so? Why not?"

Sunsets were a date activity or for tourists, neither of which applied to her. "Just haven't."

She wasn't surprised to see only one other car in the beach parking lot. "Midweek in the off-season doesn't attract a lot of sunset fans," she told him. "In the summer, this lot is much fuller."

"Our lucky night, then."

"How so?"

"We'll have privacy. I like having time alone with you."

"We've been alone all day."

"I know. I've enjoyed it." He pulled the car into a front-row space, behind the log fence that divided beach from lot. They could see the beach grass blowing in the wind. Beyond it was the silvery-brown sand and beyond that still farther, the black Atlantic with its choppy whitecaps.

"In fact…" There was the soft click of his seat belt and then Philippe was leaning just close enough for Jenna to smell his body wash and the woodsy undertones of his aftershave. "I enjoyed it very much."

Jenna's eyes fell to his lips. She knew what he was doing. He was offering her the chance to cross the line, same way she did this morning.

Her mouth and throat were suddenly dry. "The best view is on the beach," she told him.

"Are you sure, *ma chérie*? The view is quite beautiful from this vantage point." He gestured toward the ocean, but his eyes stayed on her.

"Positive. For starters, the sun sets in the west." She pointed over her shoulder. "The only thing you'll get from this view is a gray sky."

"The only thing?" The dimple in his cheek was as pronounced as ever. He definitely didn't play fair.

"By the way, you'll want to take off your shoes. The sand is very soft."

Soft and cold. Jenna forgot how quickly the grains lost their warmth when the shade moved in. She shivered as her foot sank ankle-deep into the cool dampness.

"You are going to want this as well." Philippe draped his leather jacket over her shoulders. Completely unnecessary since she was wearing a light jacket of her own, but if he wanted to play gentleman, who was she to argue? Especially when the jacket felt like having his arms around her. She pulled the leather tight and breathed in his scent.

"I will say, this is far different from Beau Rivage," Philippe remarked. "The sand is softer, and it's very peaceful."

"One of the things I love about this beach is how far removed it feels from the rest of Nantucket. It's almost like walking on a different island. Look." She pointed ahead at a trio of objects lolling on the beach. "Gray seals," she said. "There's probably more swimming around in the water just past the breakers."

"Those three look like giant gray rocks from here," Philippe remarked.

"I'm sure they appreciate the comparison. We shouldn't get too much closer. I don't want to spook them."

"Then we'll stay here." To her surprise, he sat down on the sand. "A little cold, but we will survive. If you prefer, you can sit on the jacket."

Jenna considered the supple leather wrapped around her shoulders. Much as she hated to lose the comforting scent, she'd sat on evening sand enough to know she preferred a warm bottom to extra-warm shoulders. Reluctantly, she slipped it off and spread it on the ground.

She needn't have worried, because no sooner did she take her seat than Philippe pulled her close. "To block the wind," he whispered as his arms wrapped her in a hug. "Nothing more."

Unless she chose different. Disappointment swirled in her stomach even as she appreciated the gesture. He was truly staying on his side of the line and ceding her the power. Same as he had their entire relationship. Respecting her wishes and never pushing for more.

Did he have any idea what his chivalry did to her? How giving her the space she needed to use her head actually fueled her attraction?

Handsome, charming and respectful? What woman wouldn't fall?

"What is the beach in Nice like?" She needed to focus on something other than her thoughts. "You said it was different?"

"Much. Like I said, the sand is softer here, and the water much darker. Where I spent my time, there was more development. I like how much of your coastline is open space. This is especially peaceful."

"Mmm. A few more weeks and dark this time of day." Jenna didn't know if he meant to or not, but his voice had turned soft and rhythmic, like the waves meeting the shoreline. His jaw rested against her temple, each modulated word he spoke teasing her skin. It was a struggle to keep her eyes open.

"When I first moved here, I loved how you could go to the beach any time you wanted," she told him. "Not like Boston Harbor, where going to the ocean meant visiting the piers."

"My parents loved the beach," Philippe said. "We used to go every summer as a reward for working the harvest." Jenna remembered the photo he kept on his mantel in France. She knew it was a keepsake from a happier time, but she hadn't realized it also represented the end of a tradition. Thinking of him holding on to the memory, she felt an ache in her chest.

"God, how I hated the harvest," she heard him say. He chuckled.

"You did?" Shifting in the sand, she looked to see if he was joking.

"All those hours in the sun? Who would enjoy it?" he replied. "Soon as I was old enough, my father trained me to pick the jasmine. My smaller hands would be gentle like the women we hired," he explained. "How I would curse him for sticking me with the old women. All day long telling me stories about the house and the village. I thought I would scream."

"But you love history."

"Now, yes. Wasn't until I attended university that I realized how much of those stories I had absorbed and how much I appreciated them."

"I had no idea." In her mind's eye, she imagined a young Philippe, gritting his teeth as the women chattered around him, all the time hanging on every word in spite of himself.

"Ironic, isn't it? How the things we hated as children become the things we cling to as adults."

"Like the harvest."

"*Oui*, like the harvest," he replied in a faraway voice. Jenna wondered if he was in fields of his memory. His expression always turned bittersweet when he talked of his childhood. You could feel his loss weighing down the stories.

It left her wanting to brush the weight away with her fingers.

"Is that why you come back for the harvest?"

she asked, already knowing the answer. A better question would be why he chose lavender over the fields of his childhood.

"I have to," he said. "My father, his father, his grandfather… Felix…they all worked that field. They all left part of themselves there. Every August, I feel them calling to me, and I feel too guilty not to go."

"Guilty?"

"For being the one who survived. I was the one who cared the least."

"That's not true." Jenna scrambled to her knees. With her knees pressing his jacket into the sand, she reached out and captured his face in her hands. "I've seen how seriously you take your business. I've listened to you on the phone. I watched you in the fields with the farmers. You care about that company. And when your child is born, you're going to teach her to love it, too, right down to her picking jasmine."

"Jenna, I…" It was all right if the words fell away. The moisture glistening in his eyes said it for him. Jenna brushed her thumb across his cheek. Turning his head, he nuzzled her palm before offering a smile.

"You really believe the baby will be a girl, don't you?" he asked.

"The way she demands carbohydrates? I know she is."

"Our very own Antoinette. I would like that."

While his right hand continued to hold hers, his left slipped free to splay across her abdomen. Jenna caught her breath. It was such a natural, paternal gesture, and it made her heart sing. "Part of me still can't believe it's real."

"I've got four pregnancy tests that says it is," Jenna teased. She had to make light of the moment; his touch was weaving its way into her skin. Gazing into his eyes, it was all too easy to picture a future where his hand rested on her expanded belly as the baby kicked.

"I know" was his reply. "I never doubted you for a second."

"The sun is starting to set."

The two of them turned their attention westward, where the sun was slowly disappearing behind the horizon. Only half could be seen. The remaining light painted streaks across the sky. Reds, oranges and purples blended between clouds. Jenna heard a splash, then two more as the seals headed into the Atlantic.

"Isn't it beautiful?" she said with a sigh. "Told you it was worth a drive."

"Yes," said Philippe. "Although I would have traveled anywhere if it meant holding you like this."

Jenna's heart skipped.

Little by little, the sun sank and the colors receded into black. They sat in silence, their breathing the only sounds they made. It was as if they were the only two people in the world.

"Jenna..." He didn't say anything else. Didn't have to. Jenna knew what he was asking. She took in his darkening silhouette and remembered how it felt to be in his arms. *Once more,* she thought. He wanted her, and she ached for him. She leaned in.

And kissed him.

In a flash, they were pressed hip to hip. Philippe's hands tangled in her curls as he rained kisses along her jaw and down her neck. "I've missed you, I've missed you," he murmured against her skin.

She'd missed him, too, with an intensity she hadn't realized until this moment. The ease with which she slipped under his spell frightened her, and yet it felt as natural as breathing. Which was why, when Philippe rose to his feet and held out his hand, she knew she would go with him to his hotel.

* * *

Philippe had the most vivid dream. In it, Jenna and he stood on the balcony of his apartment. Only instead of his street, the balcony looked out on an enormous field filled with crows. It must have been early morning, right after sunrise. The light was slowly spreading across the field. He stood behind her with his arms wrapped around her waist, his hands pressed to her swollen belly. Every so often the baby would kick, and he would start with amazement.

"She's a bossy one," Jenna said to him.

"Like her mother," he started to reply. But before he could finish the sentence, Jenna changed, her body turning into liquid. She flowed out of his arms and under the balcony railing.

He awoke with a start to a darkened hotel room.

"Everything all right?" Jenna's sleepy voice came to him from across the king-size bed. "You jumped in your sleep."

"Only a dream. Did I wake you?"

She made some kind of sleep noise. "My back was cold."

Immediately he rolled to his side so she could spoon against his chest. "Better?"

"Mmm…"

He lay in bed listening to the sound of her breathing. Sleep wasn't going to come back easily for him. The dream left him too tense.

Of course, he didn't need to be a psychoanalyst to parse the dream's meaning. He'd been battling a gnawing sense of anxiety since he and Jenna argued about her staying on Nantucket in the ice and snow.

If only she would return to France with him, then he wouldn't have to worry. He would be around to prevent anything happening to the baby. The two of them could experience the pregnancy together. And, if tonight was any indication, they could enjoy the physical side of their arrangement as well. Clearly their attraction hadn't waned. Unusual, but then Jenna was unusual, as evidenced by the fact he hadn't found a woman as interesting or attractive to him since her departure.

"Come back to France with me." The words poured out of him. "I would make sure you had the most wonderful pregnancy. You and the baby could have everything you wanted."

Feeling her stiffen, he pulled her closer. He'd caught her off guard.

"That must have been some dream," she said after a moment.

"I want to keep the baby safe," he told her. This was his child. The continuation of his family.

When she didn't respond, he wondered if she'd fallen asleep. "Jenna?"

"Can we talk about this in the morning?" she asked. "When you're thinking a little more clearly?"

"Of course." She had a point. The words *had* spilled out of him without much thought. There would be plenty of time for them to talk in the morning, after he'd put some distance between himself and the dream.

In the meantime, she was in his arms. He burrowed his head into the crook of her neck and willed himself to sleep.

CHAPTER NINE

"I DON'T KNOW. I just don't know where they put the cat."

"You made him sit with Lola?" Shirley remarked. Her friend was at the nursing station logging patient care information into the computer. "Are you trying to test his patience?"

As she wheeled the thermometer cart into the corner, Jenna cast a look into the activity area to where Philippe and Lola sat at one of the tables. The older woman was chattering nonsensically while nervously arranging scraps of paper into patterns. Every so often, Philippe would nod in agreement or offer a comment. "I'm sure the cat is fine," she heard him say in a voice you'd use with a young child.

Jenna's heart stuck in her throat. Patient, gentle. He was going to be a wonderful father.

"I didn't put him with anyone," she said.

"He arrived for breakfast early, and Lola latched on to him. I think she might have a little crush."

"She wouldn't be the only one," Shirley replied.

"I simply appreciate the way he is treating her. It bodes well for when the baby arrives."

"I meant the other patients on the floor. He charmed a few of them the other night when he delivered you to work. How long is he planning to hang around, anyway?"

"I don't know. He hasn't said." She left out how they'd spent her evenings off the past two nights sharing a bed. Those memories were hers alone. Besides, Shirley would read too much into things.

"But *where* is the cat?" Lola persisted. "It doesn't make sense. He was watching TV and now he's gone."

"I'm sure he'll show up," Philippe assured her. "Cats are very resilient. Maybe he went to get himself a mouse for breakfast."

"A mouse for breakfast!" Lola laughed like he'd told a joke and went back to arranging her squares. "A mouse for breakfast," she repeated, shaking her head. "That's funny."

"Lola," Jenna called over. "How about we get you cleaned up for your breakfast?"

"A mouse for breakfast," Lola called back, shaking her head again. Philippe shot them a grin.

"I don't think you're going to break them apart any time soon," Shirley said. "At least not until Lola gets her oatmeal." She leaned back in her chair. "Are you all right? You look more pale than usual."

"Apparently the pastry didn't work this morning. I'm still nauseous."

"Maybe you should tell Monsieur d'Usay to stop wining and dining you."

"He's not wining me. Alcohol is bad for the baby." Shirley had a point, though. She had been burning the midnight oil a little too much. The baby was telling her she needed to rest. When her shift ended, she'd tell Philippe she needed to take a night off and sleep. He wouldn't mind. After all, he was all about making sure baby was safe.

"You know…" She double-checked to see if Philippe was still distracted. "He asked me to go to France with him the other night."

"No way! He's persistent, I'll give him that."

"I don't think he was serious."

"Why not?"

"Because he…" *Didn't follow through in the*

morning. "I think it was more of a passing comment."

"Some passing comment. What did you say?"

"Nothing. Like I said, he really wasn't serious."

"But if he was serious…? You already told him no, right?"

"Of course." Jenna suddenly needed something to do with her hands. Picking up a pen, she began twisting the plastic cap between her fingers. "I've already made that clear, which is why I know he wasn't serious."

When was the shift change, anyway? Her stomach was churning.

Shirley give her a sideways glance before picking up a set of folders and tapping them on the desk. "Speaking of bad marriages, what does your mom think of all this?"

"You mean about the baby?"

"And the proposal."

"The proposal…" Feeling a little more in control of the subject now that Shirley was being pesky about it, Jenna set down the pen. "Is none of her business. As for the baby? She's over the moon. She keeps talking about how she and my dad are going to spoil their grandbaby rotten."

"Her and your dad, huh? They're still hot and heavy, then?"

"Oh yeah, till death do them part," Jenna replied.

"Hey, maybe the sixth time is the charm," her friend said. "You never know, right?"

"You sound like Philippe."

"Philippe knows about your parents? You don't talk about your parents to anybody."

"Philippe's different." Shirley arched a brow, forcing Jenna to grab the pen again. "I mean, crazy or not, they are the baby's maternal grandparents. The man should know what he's getting into."

"*Pardon*, ladies. I don't want to interrupt, but the two of us are going in search of a cat."

She looked up to find Philippe and Lola had left the activity room to join them at the nurses' station. The old woman was holding Philippe's hand.

"I don't know where she is," Lola said.

"I think she might be in your room," Shirley told her. "With your breakfast tray."

"Then her room shall be the first place we check," Philippe replied. Leaning over the counter, he used his free hand to tuck a curl behind Jenna's ear.

"Do not let your parents worry you so much,

ma chérie. They are going to do what they want. Foolish or not."

He'd given her the same advice last night. "I'm trying," she told him.

"I know, but their affair still bothers you. I can tell from your frown." His fingers brushed her cheek before dropping away. A whisper of a touch that had her nearly leaning forward for more. "We will talk about it more during breakfast, all right? First I must find a cat."

"Bonne chance." As she watched him walk away, Lola shuffling by his side, she thought her heart might split her chest in two.

"Oh my God."

"What?" Yanking her attention away from Philippe, Jenna saw Shirley staring with her mouth open. "What?" she repeated.

"The look on your face. You're falling for him."

"Don't be ridiculous. I was smiling at how sweet he's being with Lola."

"Uh-huh. Sure. You keep telling yourself that."

"I will," Jenna replied. Same way she would ignore the way her heart was taking up extra space in her chest with its fullness. She was not falling for Philippe. She couldn't. Because if she was falling, then she would have to take back every criticism she ever mentally hurled in her mother's direction. After all, how could she criticize someone when she was no better?

From somewhere down the hall, Lola laughed. Jenna's heart skipped a couple beats.

Oh man, she was in trouble. She wasn't falling for Philippe.

She'd already fallen.

"I finally managed to convince her that the cat was outside on holiday. Luckily, she saw a squirrel through the window and decided from the tail that I was correct."

"Are you sure it wasn't the arrival of her breakfast tray that convinced her?"

"Possibly, but I prefer to take credit."

Philippe shot her a grin before disappearing into her kitchen. A second later she heard the sound of mugs being taken out of a cupboard.

She'd been so exhausted after her shift that she asked Philippe if they could skip their breakfast in the park. With predictable protectiveness, he'd immediately brought her home and tucked her into bed so she could sleep. To her surprise, when she woke up – nearly ten hours later! — he was still there, sitting at her dining room table, typing away on his laptop.

The scene looked so incredibly right, her knees nearly buckled.

Things were so much easier when they were together in France without strings or messy emotions. When did her expectations change?

Maybe they didn't, she realized, thinking of that afternoon in Arles when they first made love. Maybe she simply didn't want to acknowledge what that connection signified.

It wasn't the baby that complicated their situation—it was her heart.

"Now what are we going to do?" Like it had all afternoon, her stomach responded with a twinge.

"Let me be the first to say that I do not like the smell of this tea."

She jumped a little at the sound of Philippe's voice. He came in from the kitchen carrying a pair of steaming mugs. "It has the base notes of a barn."

"One of the nurses at work recommended it. Says it has lots of vitamin K."

"So does romaine lettuce, but I wouldn't make a tea out of it. I made you a cup of chamomile as well in case you change your mind."

"After a sales job like that, why would I want to drink anything else?" His thoughtfulness was killing her. It'd be a lot easier to stay emotionally detached if he didn't insist on treating her like a princess.

She took a sip of tea and immediately put the mug back on the coffee table. "You're right," she said as she choked back a gag. "Barnyard."

"I told you so. Interestingly, we've had a request from Collier's for nettle leaf. They want to use it in a shampoo. I will suggest they buy a top note to go with it. And to avoid drinking it. Are you feeling better?"

"I'm not sick. Just out of sorts." She wondered if the growing realization that she was falling for the man sitting in the upholstered chair across from her was the reason. "I'm not feeling anything that isn't normal for this stage of the pregnancy." Damn. She shouldn't have said that.

You could practically see the alarm bells going off in his head. "What do you mean? What are you feeling?"

"Relax. I need to put my feet up for a little while, that's all. That's why I called in for the night." She was glossing over details, but if he got overprotective about a potential fall on the ice, she could only imagine how he'd react to hearing she felt crampy, even though she knew it was a perfectly normal feeling.

Thankfully he appeared to accept her excuse. "I've kept you up late these past couple nights," he said.

"I wasn't exactly begging to go to sleep." Bits and pieces of memories flashed through her brain, warming her cheeks. She looked over to see Philippe studying her with an amused look.

"You didn't blush on our first date," he said.

"I didn't?"

He shook his head. "No. Every one of my compliments, you took in stride. I remember being impressed that you knew your worth."

"More, I knew a line when I heard one."

"But now that we are lovers…"

Jenna blushed over the fact she could feel herself blushing. "There's an intimacy when you sleep with someone," she replied. "The compliments have more weight." She dared not say more.

"I'm glad you believe me sincere now."

Sincere about what? That he thought her beautiful? That he wanted the best for their child? "You've never been anything but honest with me."

"You make it impossible not to be. I knew when I met you that you would be judging every compliment that came out of my mouth."

Jenna laughed. "You didn't do yourself any favors by pretending to work for the hotel."

"I never pretended anything—I lied by omission. There is a difference."

"A very small one," she said. "When our daughter asks, I'm going to make sure she watches out for men like you."

"I hope so. Men like me are not to be trusted."

Sometimes they were, thought Jenna, and that made them more dangerous. She reached for her chamomile tea.

Philippe was studying his hands all of a sudden, his thumb massaging the center of his palm. It reminded Jenna of how he'd played with the wineglass the night he proposed. He was working up to something.

"There's a labor issue brewing at one of my properties. A potential work stoppage. I have to fly back to the corporate offices to oversee negotiations."

"You're leaving." Jenna's insides crumpled. *Fool.* This shouldn't be a surprise. Philippe's leaving was inevitable. She couldn't expect him to stay around Nantucket waiting on her forever. "When do you leave?"

"I fly out in the morning," he replied. "I'm sorry."

"Don't be," Jenna said. "You have a business to run. You can't stick around Nantucket doing nothing forever." Tomorrow, when he was gone, she would give herself points for keeping the disappointment out of her voice.

"If only I could. I enjoyed spending time with you again. I wish I could stay longer."

She had enjoyed spending time with him, too. "Seeing as how I didn't expect you to come to Nantucket at all, I'll take these last few days as a bonus."

So this was it. He would fly home and their affair would truly and completely be over. It was a good thing. Distance would ease the hold he had on her emotions.

A lump rose in her throat.

"You could come with me," he said suddenly.

"Back to France?"

"Why not? When negotiations are finished, we can visit Paris. You've never been to Paris, have you?"

Jenna shook her head.

"Then I could show you the city. We could have a second French holiday, so to speak."

What a wonderful, horrible idea. To what end? Wouldn't that be like pulling the bandage off slowly? Her stomach twisted at the thought.

"Ma chérie?" She must have frowned, because Philippe was across the space and at her side in a heartbeat, the concern etched on his face making the lump worse. Why couldn't he be aloof and uncaring? Why did he have to tease her with kindness and eyes that reflected emotions that weren't there? This whole situation would be so much easier.

"I—I can't take time from work. I need to save the time for when the baby comes."

"Oh." There was disappointment in his voice. "Forgive me. I didn't stop to think."

"Plus, you have no idea how long these negotiations will go. I could end up just being in the way."

"I doubt that."

"Even so, I think that maybe we should... We should say good..." She pressed a fist to her stomach.

"Jenna?"

Something wasn't right. That last cramp was stronger. Sharper.

Oh God, no. Please no.

She bolted from the room.

"Jenna?"

Philippe started down the hall after her. She rushed into the bathroom, slamming the door

behind her. Morning sickness, he decided...
That's what made her run so quickly. He didn't
want to think about what else could make her
turn so pale.

He knocked on the bathroom door. "Is everything all right?"

"Can I have a minute?" was the muffled
reply.

Definitely morning sickness. Heading back
to the living room, he sat back down in his
chair. Jenna's teacups sat on the table untouched. He picked up the nettle tea and inhaled.

"No wonder she's nauseous," he said.

Perhaps the nausea was also the reason why
she was acting so strangely. He could have
sworn that before she bolted from the room
Jenna was about to say something about goodbye.

He would ask her to explain when she returned. They were enjoying each other's company too much to simply end things. He would
be able to return to Nantucket in a few weeks,
once his business was completed. In fact, he
would no doubt be back several times over
the course of her pregnancy. They still had financial and legal issues to hammer out, and
naturally he would want to track how her preg-

nancy was going. As far as he was concerned, they could enjoy each other's company indefinitely. There was no reason for her to make their goodbye sound so permanent.

Why was she, then?

Back in France, when they were first doing their dance of attraction, she used to back away whenever the chemistry became too intense. Hide behind a wall of mistrust. There was no need to mistrust him now, though. And yet here it felt as though she was throwing up another wall.

Why did he feel he was missing something? Something important. An answer that was just out of reach?

The afghan she'd been using lay on the floor where it fell when she left the room. He bent over to pick it up. As he folded the soft pink material, he smelled the faint scent of jasmine. Closing his eyes, he inhaled deeply. Beautiful. No one wore jasmine like Jenna. The flower belonged to her. He wondered if he'd ever be able to smell the summer nights again without thinking of her.

In the distance, he heard a door followed by the sound of Jenna's footsteps as she walked into the room.

"Philippe?"

The tremor in her voice knocked him from his reverie. Opening his eyes, he found Jenna hovering in the doorway, her face paler than he'd ever seen. Even her lips were white.

His stomach dropped.

"I think we need to go to the hospital," she told him.

CHAPTER TEN

MAYBE A WIZARD put a curse on his family during the Middle Ages, or had the powers above decided the d'Usay family had spent enough time on the planet and therefore anyone attached to the name needed to go? Or had he simply done something horrible in a previous life and therefore needed to suffer punishment in this one?

Jenna was bleeding. "Not a lot," she said, but her voice had been tight and lacked conviction.

Bleeding meant miscarriage.

Philippe broke the speed laws driving them to the emergency room. There, he was forced aside while an overly chipper nurse shooed him from the room.

"We need to get her changed and then do an exam," the nurse told him. "We'll come get you as soon as we're done."

Now, with the tests and exams finished, he

returned to find Jenna lying alone in the dim light. It was midmorning, or so the clock on the wall told him. He sat by her side and held her hand while the monitor beeped out her vital signs with soft regularity.

She looked like a pale angel. Soft and delicate. The hospital gown didn't suit her— the colors were too muted. She was brighter than that.

Felix had not looked like an angel in his hospital bed. The last few weeks, his brother had looked like Nosferatu, all tight white skin and teeth.

Mama, however. She would have looked like an angel. He knew without having been there, because Mama had always insisted on looking her best.

She would have been jealous of how beautiful Jenna looked.

Jenna wasn't dying, he reminded himself.

But their child might be.

He brushed a curl from her forehead, forcing a smile when she turned her head to look at him with large, frightened eyes. "The doctor come back yet?"

"Not yet. She's on her way, the nurse outside said." His voice was surprisingly calm, considering his insides felt ready to shatter. How he hated this feeling. The hollow feeling that felt as though someone cut your insides from your heart to your stomach.

The shadow he'd spent so many years trying avoid gripped his shoulder and held on fast. This was why you didn't get involved. This was why you avoided falling in love. Because people you loved died, leaving you cold and hollow inside. Leaving you alone.

What had made him think he could escape the pain?

Jenna's lower lip trembled. "I'm scared," she said. They both were. "I've been lying here listing all the logical reasons for spotting, but it doesn't help. All I keep thinking is what if…"

"Shh. Don't say it." If they swallowed the word, perhaps it would disappear. Pressing his forehead to hers, he whispered the refrain again as if reciting a prayer. "Don't say it." His hands squeezed hers as tightly as possible, their viselike grips grounding one another. In his mind's eye, Philippe saw all the events he might never see—first steps, dances, smiles— and he prayed he was overreacting.

A knock on the door interrupted them. Looking up, he saw a woman no bigger than a girl with a gray topknot. "I am Dr. Bhattacharya," she said, her voice soft and sing-song. "How are we feeling?"

Horrible, Philippe started to say.

"Nervous," Jenna replied.

"Not surprising. I have good news, though. Your exams came back with no signs of irregularities. The cervix is intact, the uterus looks in good shape and the bleeding seems to have stopped as well."

"Oh thank God." Jenna let out a sigh of relief that Philippe could feel reverberating through her body. He wasn't quite as ready to relax. There was more that the doctor was leaving out.

"Your blood work did show that your progesterone level is low. There's a good chance that's what caused the bleeding. I'm going to prescribe a progesterone shot to see if we can boost your levels and keep this from happening again."

"But everything's going to be all right," Jenna said. "I'm not miscarrying."

"Obviously, with bleeding in early pregnancy, there's always a chance of miscarriage," Dr. Bhattacharya said. "I'm going to recommend that your ob-gyn monitors you closely just in case. But, looking at all the tests, I'm feeling good about the progesterone solving the problem."

Relief tore through him. Was it possible to lose one's breath from happiness, because he felt like all the air had rushed from his lungs in a single *whoosh*.

Thank you, he said silently. To whom, he didn't know. All he knew was they'd been given a reprieve.

"There is one more test," Dr. Bhattacharya said. She smiled at them both. "We'd like to do an ultrasound to check the baby's heartbeat."

"C-can we hear it at this point?" Jenna looked at him with excitement in her eyes. "It's not too early?"

"Shouldn't be," the doctor replied.

A few minutes later, a machine had rolled in and Dr. Bhattacharya was tracing Jenna's stomach with a wand and describing what she saw. Philippe was speechless. There, on the monitor, was his child. Tiny and hard to visualize, but more beautiful than anything he could imagine. That was, until…

"Here you go," Dr. Bhattacharya said.

Jenna gasped. "Oh my God," she whispered. "That's our baby."

It sounded like soft rapid hoof beats. Their

child's heart beat strong and sure. She was a fighter.

Like her mother. Philippe gazed at the woman beside him, awe in his heart. "*C'est beau*," he said. "Perfect."

"…you or the baby are at risk."

The doctor's words ripped him from the moment. "What did you say about risk?"

"She was talking about precautions in general," Jenna said.

"I was saying that her doctor will want to monitor her closely throughout her pregnancy to make sure neither she or the baby are at risk."

"You're saying there still could be a problem then?" Worse, Jenna could be in danger as well?

"It's just a precaution, Philippe. I'm sure they monitor pregnancies all the time."

"We do," Dr. Bhattacharya said. "We don't want to take anything for granted."

"No," Philippe replied. "You don't." Hadn't he, though? He sat back and studied the hand in his. In all his worry, he'd assumed Jenna would be all right.

What would he have done if he lost her? What would his world be like?

Dark, that's what it would be. A world devoid of color and warmth.

He couldn't let that happen. The d'Usay bad luck stopped here. Stopped now. Philippe wasn't going to lose Jenna or his child. There was only one solution: keep them close and do everything in his control to keep them safe. Starting now.

"I don't know about you, but I could use a few dozen hours of sleep." Jenna sank her head against the headrest of Philippe's rental car. Exhausted didn't begin to cover how tired she felt. "Soon as I get back to the house, I'm going to scarf down some food and take a nap."

"You will not scarf. You will have a healthy breakfast. If there is a possibility of risk, it will not be because of poor diet."

"Yes, Mother." She smiled as she said it. "Seriously, you don't have to warn me twice. I'm aiming for a picture-perfect pregnancy from here on in. The next time I visit the hospital in a rush, I want it to be because my water broke."

She ran a hand over her stomach. While she'd wanted the baby, she hadn't known how deeply that desire went until she saw the blood. Then she knew with every fiber of her being. "You hear that, baby? No more scaring your father and me, or you'll be grounded."

"Then we are in agreement. We both want to do everything possible to keep you and the baby safe."

"You are preaching to the choir. Although I feel better having talked to Dr. Bhattacharya. She knows her stuff, don't you think?"

Philippe shrugged. "She was competent."

"Well, I liked her," she replied. Philippe had been in this weird, hard-to-please mode since they left the hospital, where everything on the island bothered him. She was cutting him some slack because of the stress they'd been under.

Sunshine was beginning to breach the horizon, its orange and yellow colors mixing with fading gray. "How long were we at the hospital, anyway? The clock was behind my head and I couldn't see my... Oh my God, your flight. What time do you need to catch it?"

"Do not worry about the flight—I will reschedule."

"Thank you." In the midst of the chaos, she'd forgotten Philippe was planning to leave her. The two of them had been about to say goodbye, in fact, when the cramping hit.

Dragging out their goodbyes for another few hours might be postponing the inevitable, but Jenna was grateful anyway. "I hope it won't cause too many problems."

"They will have to deal. You and the baby come first."

Jenna was so exhausted from the ordeal that she closed her eyes and pretended the words meant more than they did.

"You really are tired," she heard Philippe say. "Once you have a few hours sleep, you can pack and we'll head to my hotel."

She pried open an eye. "Pack? For what?"

"The flight. Don't worry about packing a lot. Just the essentials will do for now. I'll have someone handle the rest."

"Whoa, back up there, cowboy." She opened her other eye and turned so she had a full view of his profile. "Where is it you think I'm going?"

"To Arles, of course."

"What?" She shook her head. "No, I said last night that I couldn't go to France with you, remember?"

"Yes, but...things are different now."

They'd reached her driveway. Unbuckling his seat belt, Philippe turned so he too was studying her. He had one elbow propped on the wheel and the other on the seat back. If he leaned forward, he could pin her in place, Jenna noted. "We both agreed we were going to do everything possible to keep the baby healthy," he said.

"Healthy, yes, but I was talking about more fruits and vegetables, not flying across the world for a vacation."

"Not vacation," he replied. "To live."

Jenna looked at him and counted to three. "I'm going to pretend you didn't say that."

She got out of the car, and he followed her across the front lawn. "The situation is different now," he said. "I realized just how much was at stake. How much I...that is, we...stand to lose."

"Don't you see?" He reached out and caught her arm. "If you come to France with me, I can make sure you have the finest doctors money can buy."

"French doctors," she replied.

"French, British, German. The best in the world. Whatever you need."

"I don't need French doctors! What I need is for you..." She stopped herself and took a deep breath. "We have perfectly adequate doctors in Nantucket."

"My child deserves more than adequate care."

"Then I'll go to Boston if I need to. Or are

you going to tell me they aren't good enough, either?"

Yanking her arm free, she stomped up the front steps. The front door was open. They'd left in such a rush, she'd forgotten to turn the latch. Great, the way things were going, there was probably a robber pilfering through her jewelry.

Philippe was two steps behind her. "*Ma chérie*, please."

"It was a scare, Philippe. Pregnant women have scares all the time, and they go on to have perfectly fine pregnancies. They don't pick up and move halfway around the world."

"People die all the time, too," he shot back.

"No one is going to die."

The entire conversation was ludicrous; she didn't know why she was even entertaining it. She headed into the kitchen, where she found the bowl of fresh fruit Philippe had brought the day before. Part of their country dinner he'd planned to make. Bread, fruit and cheese. She grabbed an orange and a knife and began slicing with vehemence.

The worst part of this stupid conversation? It wasn't that he had decided she needed to live in France, or that the basis for his decision had nothing to do with her, but rather his fear of losing the baby. No, the worst part was that she felt like an afterthought, and she hated herself for it.

A shadow fell across the doorway. "I didn't mean to upset you. When we were in the hospital, I realized—I mean, *truly* realized—how much … I don't want to lose her.… I don't want to lose…"

"I know. I don't, either. When I first saw the spotting, I thought…" Jenna's hands started to shake. The knife clattered to the counter as she pressed a trembling fist to her mouth. She would not sob. She would not…

"Shh." Philippe's hands gripped her shoulders, turning her to his chest. "It's all right."

She buried her face in his collar, letting his voice chase the tremors away. His arms were the balm she needed. The anchor. "I don't know what I would have done without you at the hospital," she said. His presence had kept her sane. She'd needed him.

She loved him.

A long, shuddering breath escaped her lips. She'd been dancing around the feeling with euphemisms for days, but now there was no escaping the truth. She loved Philippe d'Usay. She loved his child.

And he didn't love her.

Sniffing, she pulled back. "You're going to need a clean shirt," she said. The collar was wet where she'd buried her face.

"I have plenty of shirts." He kissed the top of her head. "Why don't you sit down and rest and I will bring you a proper breakfast. I will impress you with my culinary skills," he said, guiding her to a kitchen chair.

She let out a watery laugh. "You already impress me."

"*Mon Dieu*, it's a miracle. And here I have yet to crack an egg. How far we've come from that day on the terrace when you thought me a threat to your virtue."

"I considered you a playboy who went through women like water," she countered.

"'Like water' is an exaggeration. I like to think I am more selective than that."

Jenna noticed he didn't say *was*.

Perhaps she was being childish by playing games with semantics, but words counted. For as long as she could remember, she'd promised herself that when she fell in love, she would pick someone kind, considerate and devoted. Most importantly, however, she would fall for someone as far removed from her father as possible. Leave it to her to fall for a kind, considerate playboy. Words reminded her, during moments like this, that while Philippe was a part of her life, he was not committed to her.

"Fried or scrambled?"

"Scrambled."

"Excellent choice. My fried eggs are horrible. You know," he said, kicking the refrigerator door shut, "when you come to France, we can do this every morning."

She looked up from the orange rind she was playing with. "What's that? Cry over fruit?"

"Eat scrambled eggs."

"We have scrambled eggs in New England."

His face darkened, and he turned around. A second later, she heard the crack of an egg against the bowl. "I have lost every person in my life who has ever mattered to me. I can't lose any more."

The naked vulnerability in his voice punched her right in the heart. She wasn't trying to hurt him. Couldn't he see that? She was trying to protect herself. "This baby means everything to me, too," she told him.

The baby she carried was part of Philippe which made her as precious to Jenna as her own life. "I would never let anything happen to her."

"I know, but…"

"But what?"

He turned around. "You'll be halfway around the world. There's only so much flying back and forth that I can do. There are too many people depending on me to be in France."

"I understand."

"But I want to be there. I want to be a part of everything. I want to hear the baby's heartbeat, see the ultrasound." His face grew wistful. "Watch her smile for the first time. Share her first Christmas."

In other words, he wanted to be a father. A true, hands-on father.

He knelt in front of her, hands grasping the sides of her chair. "That is why I want you to come to France," he said. "So we can share these moments together."

"Be a family," Jenna whispered. Philippe painted a beautiful picture, prettier than any Provençal landscape. There was only one piece missing from his scenario.

She stared at the buttons on his shirt, thinking how smooth and starched he looked despite a night in the emergency room. She tried to image the same starchiness holding an infant as she cried and dribbled formula. He probably wouldn't show a wrinkle. To the outside world, Philippe d'Usay would never look less than perfect.

"Tell me something." Slowly, she lifted her eyes. "In this family picture, where are the baby and I when you have a date?"

At least he had the courtesy to look shocked at the question. "*Pardon*?"

"Would we be upstairs out of sight, or are we going to be super cosmopolitan about the whole thing and double-date and stuff?" With that, she pushed herself out of the chair and headed into the living room. Her teacups from the night before were still on the coffee table, half-full. Picking up the nettle tea, she gave it a sniff, smiling sadly at the barnyard smell.

"What are you talking about?" Philippe asked.

"You and your 'selective' lifestyle," she replied. "A family—a real family—is based on mutual commitment and love. You've made it very clear you don't believe in either."

"Perhaps I've changed."

Jenna nearly dropped the cup. "Changed how?"

"What if I told you I'm just as afraid of losing you as I am the baby?" Taking the cup from her hands, he set it on the table. "There's three parts to a family, Jenna. The baby, the father and the mother." As he spoke, he traced a shape on her palm with his finger. "I cannot imagine my family without you as the third part. Our world would be very dark without you, Jenna Brown. My world would be dark. *Je t'aime.*"

She didn't know what to say. His world would be dark? How she'd longed to hear words like that come out of his mouth. Her heart leaped with happiness.

Her head, however... She stepped back just as Philippe leaned in for a kiss. He ended up stumbling slightly and stubbing his shin on the coffee table.

"Leopards don't change their spots, Philippe," she told him.

Lines of confusion marked his forehead. "What does that mean?"

"It means..." That it took having his back against the wall for him to declare his feelings.

Turning her back to him, she crossed from the sofa to the window. It was light enough now that she could see her backyard. The foliage had turned, she noted. The leaves on her maple had become a kaleidoscope of yellow and orange. New England foliage was beautiful until you had to rake it up.

She played with the hem of her gingham

curtain. "It means that you had a horrible scare tonight, and I think that you will say anything to make sure you have as full a role as possible in this baby's life."

Silence. The air grew thick. She could feel Philippe's eyes at the back of her head. Pictured how they widened before darkening with offense.

"Is that how you really feel?" he asked.

Jenna continued to look out the window.

"Your silence says everything. If you don't believe me, I don't know what I can say to convince you." There were footsteps as he walked across the room. Moving away, not closer. "You should get some rest," he said.

"Where are you going?"

"To my hotel. I… I need to change my travel arrangements, and we obviously could use the space. Hopefully these negotiations will not take long, and I can return soon."

"Don't."

She turned around. Philippe stood in the doorway, wearing a hopeful expression. It was clear he thought she wanted him to stay. "Don't keep flying in and out."

His face fell. "You're cutting me out?"

"No." She didn't want to keep him from being a part of the baby's life—she simply wanted to protect her heart. "I'll let you know when there are important appointments so you can attend. But I can't have you coming and going without warning. It's too…"

"Much like your father?" he asked.

His comment brought her up short. "I was going to say disruptive. What on earth does my father have to do with anything?"

"The way he pops in and out of your mother's life."

"You think I'm comparing our situation to theirs?"

Philippe folded his arms. "I don't know, *ma chérie*. Are you?"

"You're out of your mind."

"Am I? Since the day we met, I have had to fight to gain your trust."

"That's not true," Jenna said.

"Oh, but it is. You held yourself back from day one. Always wary, always waiting for me to prove I was a cad. I needed to take two steps forward for you to take one. And now I lay my soul bare and you don't believe me. So tell me, Jenna, who are you comparing me to, if not your father?"

Jenna glared at him. Thanks to their argument, she never got her eggs—a promise Philippe failed to keep—and now she had a raging headache. The last thing she needed was his attempt at armchair psychology. And on top of it, to paint himself as the victim? Give her a break.

"First off," she said, stabbing the air with her index finger, "you didn't 'lay your soul bare.' You decided I was moving to France for the baby's sake."

"And yours," he shot back. "Were you not listening? I told you how much you mean to me."

"Only as an afterthought. You wouldn't have mentioned your feelings at all if I hadn't pressed the issue."

"That is not true."

"Isn't it?" she asked. "You weren't exactly professing undying love."

"Do not presume to know my thoughts."

"Then don't presume to know mine!" Her shout hung between them. Philippe ran a hand through his hair.

"What are you afraid of, Jenna? We could have something good. A true family."

Until you broke your promise and left us alone.

Left her alone.

The world would be a lot better if people used their heads instead of their hearts.

Wasn't that what Philippe said the other afternoon? Well, she was using her head.

"I think you better leave," she told him.

"Jenna…" He took a step forward. Jenna held her breath. Her resolve wasn't as strong as she made it out to be. One kiss, one impassioned *please* and it would shatter. *Convince me I'm wrong*, she pleaded with him silently. *Change my mind.*

"I'll let you know my travel itinerary as soon as I know it." Turning on his heel, he walked away. Leaving Jenna alone.

"At least my father says goodbye when he leaves," she whispered.

CHAPTER ELEVEN

HE'D DONE THE right thing, Philippe told himself. Walking away. If he had stayed, he would have lost his temper. A leopard didn't change his spots, indeed.

Heaving a groan, he threw himself facedown on his hotel bed. Why was she being so stubborn? He was offering her a wonderful life. A home, a family. *Mon Dieu*, he'd told her he loved her!

And what had she done? Spat it back into his face. Suggested he was lying to get his way.

Only after your back was against the wall.

Argh! He flipped over onto his back. When they left the hospital, he'd been consumed with worry. Making sure Jenna and the baby came home were foremost in his mind. He intended to tell her his feelings, but then they started arguing about France and the conversation got away from him. But he did tell her eventually.

Je t'aime. I love you. Even a woman who didn't speak French had to know what he meant. And if she didn't understand, hadn't he implied his feelings enough? After all, he'd told her he couldn't lose another person whom he loved. Wasn't the meaning obvious?

She hadn't said she loved him back.

A hole opened in his chest, the pain ripping through him. Reminding him he was, again, alone with no one to love him in return.

Jenna, with her wary wall, had a point. In fact, he knew she was right. He should have listened to his own advice and walked away as soon as Jenna started slipping under his skin. Instead, like a fool, he kept coming back for more.

Perhaps if he had, his chest wouldn't feel so battered and empty. Turns out he didn't need someone to die to feel alone.

The biggest irony of all? After years of protecting his heart from pain, he was destroyed by a woman who played the game better.

Jenna sighed and began counting the syringe kits for the third time. No one ever mentioned the downside of keeping your pride. Dignity might let you walk with your head held high, but it also left you with a six-foot-two hole in your heart.

"At least I've got you," she said to her belly. Baby, at least, seemed to be doing better. There hadn't been any more spotting or cramping, which was good. In fact, she noticed today her pants were too snug.

"You look a million miles away." Shirley joined her behind the counter, a stack of admission papers in her hand. "Everything okay?"

Far from it. Everything was blown to smithereens.

"I had to use an elastic band to button my pants this morning," she said out loud.

"Because of the baby or the breakfast treats?"

"That's not funny."

Her friend held up a hand. "Sorry. Didn't realize that was a sticking point now."

No, Jenna was the one who was sorry. Shirley didn't know that talk of pastry poked at the hole in her heart.

At least she was at work. She refused to waste her time crying over what might have been. Give the sting a couple days to fade and she'd be fine. Alone, but fine.

"Oh, for crying out loud." She started counting the syringe kits *again*. "I've forgotten how to count to ten. Stupid baby brain."

Shirley gave her a look but fortunately decided to keep any comments to herself. "We've got a new patient arriving this afternoon," she said. "Coming over from the hospital to go on hospice."

"And so goes the circle of life," Jenna replied. "We live, we die and in between we struggle not to make fools of ourselves."

"Wow, thanks for the wisdom, Miss Sunshine."

"Sorry. I don't mean to be witchy. I'm just tired." Despite being exhausted, she hadn't slept very much. Another reason why she was unable to count the kits.

Shirley slid the kits to her side of the desk. "What happened?" When Jenna finished explaining, her friend practically pushed her into a chair. "Oh, Jenna. I'm so sorry! What are you doing at work on your feet, you idiot?"

"I'm fine," Jenna replied, slapping her friend's hands away. "Work won't hurt me. Besides, I need to keep my mind occupied."

"And how's that working out for you?" Shirley asked. She pointed to the saline bags that were still uncounted.

"How do you think?"

"I can't believe he walked out like that—and that you let him."

"What was I supposed to do? Beg him to stay?"

Their final goodbye wouldn't stop haunting her. Every time she closed her eyes, she saw the look on Philippe's face when he said goodbye. The light in his eyes faded away, leaving them dark and shuttered. "If he wanted to stay, he would have."

"Oh, sure—totally," Shirley drawled. "I know I would stay if I told someone I loved them and they threw it back in my face."

Not her, too. Philippe painting her as the bad person she understood. Didn't like, but understood. Shirley was supposed to be on her side, though. "He didn't say he loved me. He said he needed me to make a family."

"He didn't say anything else?"

"Something in French that was probably supposed to be romantic, I'm not sure."

"Do you remember what it was?"

"Does it really matter?" He was gone. Probably caught the first flight he could get.

"No, but I'm curious," Shirley said. "I never got to try out my French immersion software, and I want to see if it stuck."

Jenna shook her head. She really wasn't planning to get into a word-for-word recap. It hurt too much. "Jet something."

"Was it *je t'aime*?"

"I think so."

"You idiot!" Her friend smacked her on the shoulder with a force that sent her chair rolling backward. "That's 'I love you' in French."

He'd said the words? Jenna's heart started to skip until common sense shut it down. "It doesn't matter. People say 'I love you' all the time and don't mean it."

"Some of them do."

"Yeah, well, he also meant it when he said he had no intention of ever marrying or having a family, and there is a lot more evidence to support that claim."

"True," Shirley replied. "I mean, he only flew halfway across the world so he could bring you breakfast and hang out with your dementia patients." She waved to Lola, who was straightening magazines in the entertainment room. "Oh, and spent the night in the emergency room holding your hand."

"Because the baby is important to him. She—it—means the continuation of his family line. What?" Shirley had rolled her eyes.

"You just said he had no intention of ever having a family. Clearly he does if that baby matters."

"The baby's name." But even as she snapped

the response, Jenna knew that wasn't true. The baby mattered very much, so much he'd wanted her to go to France so he could keep an eye on her pregnancy.

Because he wanted a family. Something he claimed to never want. Was it possible she was wrong? Or did wishful thinking have her hearing what she wanted?

"Did you know that Philippe accused me of having daddy issues?"

"Seriously?"

"Yeah. He said I didn't trust him because I lumped him in with my father, or something to that effect."

Her friend started counting the syringe kits.

"Don't tell me you agree with him," Jenna said.

"Well, you don't really trust men," Shirley replied. "Whenever we go out, you shoot down most of the guys who talk to you."

"With good reason."

"I'm not saying you don't have reason. I'm just saying you don't trust many of the guys you meet."

"Because I've seen the damage the wrong guy can do."

"You mean guys like your dad," Shirley replied.

"I…" She didn't want to have this conversation anymore. "I'm going to go down to the front desk to see if Nelo knows anything more about our new patient," she said.

Shirley took the hint. "Suit yourself. There are eleven kits. You're welcome."

Daddy issues. She did not compare every man to her father. Jenna marched around the workstation to the elevator. Before she could push the button, however, the doors slid open to reveal the very man they'd been discussing.

Jenna's heart stopped. What was he doing here? "I—I thought you were going home."

He was dressed for business in a dark suit and cashmere coat. The same outfit he wore his first morning on the island, only this time he had the benefit of a fresh shower and shave. Thankfully sunglasses covered his eyes, meaning she didn't have to see his shuttered gaze again.

"I am." The flatness in his voice made her cringe. "I should have departed earlier, but …" He shook his head. "Never mind."

He had a gift bag in his had. "I wanted to drop this off before I left," he said, handing it to her.

Jenna didn't know what to say; she was too focused on the idea of him leaving. Taking the bag, she looked at it and saw the gift label read "For Lola."

"You're bringing a present for Lola?"

"Something I promised last time I was here. I didn't want her to think I forgot."

It was more likely Lola had forgotten the conversation and the promise. "She's in the entertainment room if you want to give her the present yourself," she said.

"Thank you, but I cannot stay. I have a conference call in an hour. I thought…" Once again, he shook his head. "Tell Lola I said goodbye."

Still no goodbye for her.

"Philippe, please." She stopped him from boarding the elevator again. "I… I'm sorry."

"Are you really?" he asked.

"Yes. I don't want us to part with unsettled business."

"But you still want to part." When she went to speak, he held up a hand. "You don't have to elaborate. I accept your apology."

"Thank you." She waited for the relief to arrive and free the tension from her shoulders, but it didn't come.

"When do you leave?" she asked him.

"I have a flight out of Boston this afternoon. I leave the island at ten."

Five hours from now. He'd be gone for real this time. No miraculous appearance off the elevator. Her heart sank even as she reminded herself the decision to stay behind had been hers.

"The…um…that is… I spoke to my ob-gyn yesterday. She suggested I have an ultra-sound next month. I will let you know when it's scheduled, in case you decide you want to attend."

"You know I will."

Jenna nodded. Was this to be their new nor-mal? Awkward, cordial conversation about tests and appointment dates? A lump the size of a boulder rose in her throat. "I guess I should let you go, then," she said. "I don't want you to miss your call."

"Merci."

"Philippe, wait!" Once again, she stopped him from stepping on the elevator. "Can I at least get a goodbye?" she asked, hating her-self a little for the request, but needing the closure more.

A look crossed his face, and then he nod-ded. *"Oui.* Of course."

He combed his fingers into her hair, the way he did when they made love, and lifted her face to his. Jenna looked into his eyes, hoping for one more look into their deep violet depths, but the sunglasses kept them hidden. She pictured them anyway, the image seared into her memory.

Dipping his head, he kissed her softly. Sweetly. Too sweet for her tastes. Clutching his shoulders, she deepened the kiss, workplace professionalism be damned.

"*Je t'aime, ma chérie*," he whispered when they parted.

"I…" *Say it*, her heart urged. *Tell him.*

The words stuck in her throat. No longer able to look him in the eye, she focused on the base of his throat. "I'm sorry," she whispered.

His Adam's apple bobbed up and down. "So am I."

Ignoring the look on Shirley's face, Jenna turned around and walked past the nurses' station to the entertainment room.

"For me?" Lola's eyes lit up with surprise when Jenna handed her the bag. "What is it?"

"I don't know. You'll have to open it to find out." It was hard to speak while holding back tears, but she managed.

Lola tossed the bright blue tissue paper on the floor and let out a laugh. "That's why I couldn't find him! He was in the bag!" She pulled out a stuffed gray and white cat.

* * *

"I was just thinking about Beatrice," Shirley said as they were leaving work a short while later.

Jenna was only half listening. Her mind was still at the elevator hearing Philippe whisper *I love you*. The reply had been right there in her throat. All she had to do was say it aloud. Why couldn't she? Why couldn't she trust that Philippe's whispers meant something? Meant forever.

"What made you think about her?" she asked.

Her friend shrugged as she burrowed through her pocketbook. "I don't know. You and Philippe and how her inheritance was the reason you met him in the first place. Makes me wonder what she'd say about this whole mess."

"Probably something like 'don't worry about what anybody else thinks,'" Jenna replied.

"Maybe." Pulling out her car keys, the blonde pressed the auto-lock button. A few feet away, her SUV's lights flashed. "She ever talk to you about her husband?"

"Her partner in crime? All the time. Called him the love of her life."

The conversation was making Jenna's tears

threaten again. Bad enough she had to fight them back every time Lola showed her that stuffed cat.

"Did you know she once told me that marrying him was the greatest adventure of her life?" Shirley said.

Jenna nodded. Beatrice had shared the same memory with her several times. "What's your point?"

"No point," her friend replied. "I think it's interesting, though, that she considered marriage her greatest adventure, and then left you money to have an adventure of your own. Makes you wonder what she really wanted you to do."

"I doubt she expected me to meet Philippe." Beatrice was awesome, but she wasn't psychic.

Shirley opened her driver's door. "True. On the other hand, it does make you wonder if she thought you should take a chance on something more than a trip to France."

Suddenly Jenna got the point of the conversation. "Subtle."

"Don't blame me," her friend replied. "Blame Beatrice. Call me later if you feel like talking."

Jenna's phone began to buzz the second she shrugged off her coat. Kicking herself because her first thought was about Philippe, she checked the call screen. Not Philippe. Or Shirley, either. It was her mother.

The two of them hadn't talked for a couple of days. The last thing Jenna was in the mood to hear about was her parents' extramarital affair with one another.

She could only ignore the inevitable for so long, though. Sooner or later, she would need to talk to the woman.

"Hi, Mom," she said as she lay down on the sofa. "What's new?"

A gut-wrenching cough answered her greeting. "Sorry," her mother croaked.

Awesome. They could be miserable together. Jenna waited until her mother caught her breath before talking. "You sound horrible."

"I feel worse. This will teach me for waiting on my flu shot. How are you feeling?"

"Just got home from work." No sense telling her about the hospital visit. There was nothing the woman could do at this point. And she definitely wasn't going to tell her about Philippe.

Instead she forced herself to ask her next question. "Dad taking good care of you? Bringing you hot tea, crackers and all that?"

Even if her mother hadn't paused, Jenna

would have guessed her response. "You know your father. He doesn't do well with sickness," she said. "Plus he needs to keep his distance so he doesn't get sick, too. Things are crazy busy at work for him. Lots of business dinners…"

"His new inventory manager attending these dinners, too?" she asked.

"Your father works with all sorts of people, Jenna."

In other words, yes. Looked like this reunion would be shorter than usual. Maybe it was because she was emotionally drained, but she couldn't stomach the excuses anymore. "Why do you take him back? He does this to you every single time."

"I love him," her mom said simply.

"But he doesn't love you."

"That's not true. He tells me he loves me all the time."

"Then turns around and leaves you home sick while he goes out to dinner." *And dumps you as soon as he finds a replacement.* "Actions speak louder than words, Mom. When's the last time he did something nice for you, or anyone, for that matter?"

"You don't understand. Your father has a lot of people demanding things of him. The last thing he needs is me distracting him with a lot of whiny demands. I'm lucky he spends as much time with me as he does."

It was the same load of bogus excuses her mother gave every time. "All I'm saying is that maybe there's someone out there that's better than Dad. Someone who… I don't know… sticks around."

Someone who wants to build a family, a voice said in her head.

On the other end of the line, her mother sniffed—and it wasn't from the flu. "I didn't call to hear a lecture about relationships from my single-mother daughter. Your father and I are back together, and that's that."

"Fine," Jenna said. She didn't want to have this conversation, either. Her mother was going to stay in her bubble of delusion forever, and there was nothing Jenna could do. Some things never changed.

Pleading a headache, she told her mother she'd call her back and let the phone drop on the floor.

"Your grandmother's in love with a loser," she told the baby. "How on earth a woman can be so blind to the obvious is beyond me. I mean, the guy's taking his girlfriend out while she's home with the flu. All I did was complain about feeling tired and your daddy made me two different kinds of tea."

Actions speak louder than words...

Her father would never bring her mother pastry or hang out at a nursing home hunting for an invisible cat. God knew he'd never fly across the world for her.

Or move heaven and earth to keep her safe.

How on earth could Philippe have thought she was comparing him to her father? There was no contest. Her father was a bastard. Philippe...

Loved her.

The awareness of it hit her like a ton of bricks. Philippe loved her. All this time she'd been afraid of falling in love with a man who didn't love her, and he was saying it every day. With every pastry, every neck rub. She'd simply been too blind—or too scared—to see the truth.

But Philippe wasn't scared. Philippe, who in his own words had lost everyone he ever loved, was brave enough to love her.

She pressed her hand to her stomach. "What have I done, baby?"

Ten past ten. Philippe checked his watch against the clock behind the concierge desk.

The times were identical. If he didn't leave soon, he would miss his flight to Boston.

Maybe two more minutes.

Why bother? He already delayed his departure a day on the chance Jenna would knock on his door. Now he was stretching out his ultimatum. It was time to accept that Jenna wasn't coming. He didn't know what made him foolish enough to think that she might. Hope was a very stupid emotion.

No more.

From now on, whatever love was left in his heart belonged to his child. For as long as she was in his life. A bitter, gloomy thought, he knew. It appeared the brooding he'd spent his life fighting had won the battle. Why not? He was tired of the struggle. His heart didn't feel like pretending it wasn't broken.

The doorman approached with his keys. "Your rental car is parked out front, Mr. d'Usay. I put your bag in the trunk."

"I hope you enjoyed your stay at the Merchant Seafarer," he added when Philippe handed him a tip.

"You have an excellent hotel." Thankfully the man didn't ask if he'd had a pleasant stay, saving Philippe from having to make up a suitable answer. "Could you leave a message for

Mr. Merchant letting him know I will email him soon?"

"Absolutely, sir. Have a good trip."

Nodding his goodbye, Philippe made his way through the front door. True to the doorman's word, his car was parked and running a few feet down the curb.

He was reaching for the door handle when he heard the sharp blare of a car horn, followed by another. Three, in fact, in rapid succession. Looking up, he saw a red sedan barreling up the hotel driveway.

It was Jenna. She stopped the car next to his.

"What are you doing?" he hollered as she leaped from the driver's seat. Driving like a maniac. Didn't she know she could have an accident?

"We were afraid we'd be too late," she said.

Too late for… His jaw dropped in disbelief. Was she saying what he thought she was saying? He was afraid to guess; all his other assumptions had been wrong.

But it was there. In eyes warmer and greener than he'd ever seen. Like the color of plants in the spring.

"*Iloveyou*," she said, the words rushing out as one. "I love you, Philippe d'Usay."

"Are you sure?" He was almost afraid to believe what he was hearing.

"Yes. I think I have loved you from the moment we met, but I was too scared—too stupid—to let myself feel it."

Listening to her words, it felt as though the sun burst through the clouds. The fullness in his heart chased away the darkness. "I love you, too."

"I know." She gave him a watery smile. "And I am so very sorry I didn't believe you. I was wrong the other day. I didn't understand…"

Oh dear God. The French. He was such an idiot. "I should have told you in English."

"No, that's not it. I didn't understand what love looked like. I thought love was something people talked about, but it's not. It's something you do."

With a shaking hand, she took his and pressed it to her stomach. "I want to show this baby what love really is. I want us to be a family. The next generation of d'Usays." She gazed up through damp lashes. "If you'll have me."

They were the most beautiful words he'd ever heard. "Oh, *ma chérie*, you've had me since the day on the terrace. I love you. I will always love you."

"Then that's all I need to hear."

Philippe too. Wrapping her in his arms, he held her tight. Heart to heart. He would never let her go.

"Take me home," she whispered in his ear.

A wonderful request, but he needed to make sure of her answer. "Which home is that?" he asked.

Her face beamed with love. "Wherever you are, my love. Wherever you are."

CHAPTER TWELVE

July

If you send me one more photo, I will kill you.

Just trying to show you what you're missing. Hurry up and get here. Your bedroom is waiting.

Forget the bedroom. I want a big bottle of French wine. You and I are seriously overdue for a celebration. You owe me for cutting me out of the wedding.

JENNA LAUGHED. SHIRLEY had been on her about the wedding since she broke the news. Upset that she didn't get to be maid of honor.

You're coming to the reception. Isn't that enough?

The wedding, by mutual choice, had been a private affair. Since she'd been six months along at the time, Jenna hadn't wanted an elaborate event. Of course, as Philippe pointed out, if she'd married him the first half dozen times he proposed, she would have been earlier in her pregnancy. But Jenna had held out for Valentine's Day. There was something poetic about pledging your heart on the most romantic day of the year. She, who had always viewed hearts and flowers with cynicism.

But, while the ceremony had been intimate, Philippe's position required some kind of public celebration, and so they were having a formal reception that weekend at the château. Shirley, who was finally getting her trip to France, had landed in Paris that morning.

Hey, did I mention Philippe has some really cute employees?

Shut your mouth. Joe's already paranoid I'll meet a sexy Frenchman and run away.

Hey, it happens. Maybe we can send him a few photos. Make him jealous enough to propose.

Listen to you…all romantic. What happened to the cynical girl I know and love?

She went to France. And decided to take a chance on love.

All thanks to Beatrice. Her thoughts traveled back a year, to when the old woman was still alive. One night she hadn't been able to sleep, so Jenna sat with her looking at old photographs. Picture after picture of Beatrice and her husband on their many trips.

"You had an amazing time together," Jenna had told her.

The woman had set down the album and taken Jenna's hand. "We live, we die, but in between we have to live," she'd said. "I got to live a lot. You should, too."

Jenna was glad she'd taken Beatrice's advice.

She took in the fields below. Once again, nature had created a magnificent tapestry of purple, green and yellow. It would be harvest time shortly. The air was already heavy with the sweet smell of lavender. Had it really been a year since the first time she saw these fields? The time had flown by.

"Someone missed you," Philippe announced.

He stepped onto the terrace, looking very domestic with a cloth towel draped over one shoulder and a sleeping baby on the other. Jenna's breath caught as it always did when she saw him.

"You're sexy when you change diapers," she told him. "Did you know that?"

"I know that is a shameless ploy to try and make me change more." He leaned in and kissed the spot behind her ear. "Did you reach Shirley?"

"Uh-huh. She's on her way."

"And your mother?"

"About thirty minutes ahead of Shirley." Her parents' reconciliation had managed to last three months before imploding. As usual, her mom was handling the breakup poorly. But she had agreed to attend the reception, so maybe things were looking up. Maybe the Brown habit of finding love in France would rub off on her. A girl could hope, anyway.

"It will be very interesting having this place filled with people again," Philippe said. "There hasn't been a proper party since my parents died. It feels good."

Yeah, thought Jenna, it did. She rested her head on her husband's shoulder. "Do you think your family would have liked me?"

"Are you kidding? *Chérie*, they would have loved you more than I do, if that's possible. And they would have adored our little prince."

As if on cue, Felix Antoine d'Usay began to whimper. "I told you he missed his mother," Philippe said. "Here you go, my son."

He placed the squirming child in her arms, pausing to adjust the sun hat that covered Felix's head. "And you thought we were having a girl."

"So I predicted wrong and gave you a son to carry forth the d'Usay name. Are you complaining?"

"Absolutely not." His kissed her, and together they smiled down at the child in her arms. Jenna had never been happier.

It was going to be a wonderful adventure.

* * * * *

Welcome to the
Destination Brides quartet!

Summer Escape with the Tycoon
by Donna Alward
Swept Away by the Venetian Millionaire
by Nina Singh
One Night in Provence
by Barbara Wallace

And look out for the final book
Coming soon!

If you enjoyed this story,
check out these other great reads
from Barbara Wallace

Their Christmas Miracle
Christmas with Her Millionaire Boss

Both available now!